Dear Diary,

I hate my life. I don't know how this happened. I turned into exactly the kind of person I have loathed my entire life. How, how could it have happened? Sometimes I wonder, if I had stayed friends with Sam and Carrie, would everything have turned out differently? Can friendship really have that kind of power? How could I have let all my dreams just slip away?

I wonder what ever became of Sam and Carrie. I haven't heard from either of them in years. Did their dreams come true?

Emma

Sunset Fantasy

CHERIE BENNETT

Sunset™
Island

SUNSET FANTASY is an original publication of
The Berkley Publishing Group.
This work has never appeared before in book form.

SUNSET FANTASY

A Berkley Book / published by arrangement with
General Licensing Company, Inc.

PRINTING HISTORY
Berkley edition / October 1994

A GLC BOOK

Splash and *Sunset Island* are trademarks belonging to
General Licensing Company, Inc.

ISBN: 0-425-14458-5

BERKLEY®
Berkley Books are published by
The Berkley Publishing Group,
200 Madison Avenue, New York, New York 10016.
BERKLEY and the "B" design
are trademarks belonging to Berkley Publishing Corporation.

PRINTED IN THE UNITED STATES OF AMERICA

10 9 8 7 6 5 4 3 2 1

To Amanda Hedleston of Culpeper, Virginia, the winner of the Sunset Island story contest. Her story idea was the inspiration for this book.

(Hey, it takes a really special girl to knock Jeff off the ol' dedication page!!)

ONE

"Yo, Carrie, lighten up!" Samantha Bridges exclaimed to her best friend, Carrie Alden. "What is the biggie? It's not like he asked you to lie down in the middle of the dance floor and do the wild thing! He asked you to dance! It's totally legal, it's moral, and it's not fattening!" Sam shook her wild red hair back over her shoulders for emphasis, narrowly missing a waitress balancing about a dozen beer bottles on a tray.

"Oh, very funny," Carrie commented dryly.

"I mean it, Car," Sam insisted vehemently, "you've got to snap out of it and stop being such a wuss!"

"Look, just because I didn't want to dance with some guy I've never met before does not make me a wuss," Carrie protested.

"Sheesh," Sam replied under her breath. She glanced around the packed Play Café to see if she could spot their other best friend, Emma Cresswell. Instead she caught a glimpse of the guy who'd just asked Carrie to dance. He was out on the tiny café dance floor with some other girl. "Well, too late for you and that hunk-o-burnin' love now," Sam teased. "He asked some other babe to dance."

"You thought he was cute, huh?" Carrie asked Sam.

"Major," Sam replied significantly.

"Good, you go dance with him, then," Carrie said.

"He didn't ask me," Sam pointed out, glancing at the Mickey Mouse watch she was wearing. "Not that I'd let that stop me, of course." She looked up and gave a brief wave to the guy. Sure enough, he shot a glance at her.

2

"You amaze me," Carrie said with a laugh.

"I know," Sam agreed. "Sometimes I amaze me, too. Oh, there's Emma!" Sam raised her long arm and waved frantically. "She's looking for us at our usual table instead of over here at the bar." She waved again and finally caught Emma's eye.

"Hi," Emma said, squeezing in next to Carrie. "Why are you guys sitting here?"

"Because tonight we're wild women," Sam retorted, and wiggled her eyebrows at Emma.

"She's a wild woman all the time," Carrie told Emma. "Actually, all the tables were full when we got here."

"Hey, see that cute guy with the auburn hair over there dancing with the blonde?" Sam asked Emma over the raucous music. "He just asked Carrie to dance."

Emma looked at Carrie. "You said no?"

"Of course she said no," Sam answered for Carrie. "She's like a nun while Billy's gone." Sam studied the guy as he danced. "Who is he?"

"Who knows, who cares?" Carrie asked blithely.

Sam sighed. "Sometimes I worry about you, girl."

"Hey, she's in love and her love is in Seattle," Emma reminded Sam lightly.

"Well, if you can't be with the one you love, love the one you're with, I always say!" Sam exclaimed.

"Big talk," Carrie teased her. "You and Pres are together again and you are true blue."

Sam smiled just thinking about Presley Travis, her boyfriend. He was tall and rangy, with long blond hair he wore tied back in a ponytail, and he had the cutest Tennessee twang to his voice. *He's also smart and nice and kind and he loves me,* Sam thought happily. *At least I think he loves me. Or I mean, I hope he loves me. . . .*

"I don't think any of the guys in here are as cute as Pres," Emma told Sam. "So what's the point of flirting?"

"You guys know I consider flirting an art form!"

"And you paint a masterpiece nightly!" Carrie said with a grin.

"Yeah," Sam agreed. "Hey, we're young and single. We live on a resort island, it's summer, and there are, like, two stud-muffins for every babe in here! On top of that . . . we are major league cute tonight, don't you think?"

Blond-haired, perfectly groomed Emma had on a plain white T-shirt with a low-cut back over white baggy cotton pants with a drawstring waist; fresh-faced brunette Carrie had on jeans and a hot pink Sunset Island T-shirt; and wild red-haired Sam—in her usual totally original Sam style—had on an old-fashioned cotton and ribbon camisole she'd found at a thrift store with short cutoff jeans and her trademark red cowboy boots. The camisole had holes in it, and each hole had been backed with different remnants of see-through lace.

"Actually, that outfit is pretty tame for you," Emma told her.

5

"Huh, I must be losing my edge," Sam remarked.

As the three of them chatted on, the Play Café got more crowded by the minute—it was *the* evening hangout on Sunset Island, the famous resort island off the coast of Portland, Maine, where Sam, Emma, and Carrie were working as au pairs for their second summer. They'd met the summer before, when Sam and Emma were eighteen and Carrie was seventeen, and they'd had such amazing adventures and had so much fun together that they'd all decided to return.

Actually, all three girls were amazed that they had become friends at all. They were so different from one another. Sam Bridges was tall and model-thin. She was raised in the small town of Junction, Kansas, and she dreamed of becoming rich and famous. Sooner rather than later. In fact, she'd quit college to follow her dream of becoming a great dancer— although it hadn't exactly worked out. Recently she had begun designing clothes for a local boutique on the island.

Carrie Alden was as down to earth as Sam was wild. Medium height, brown haired, and curvy—*too* curvy, Carrie thought—she was girl-next-door attractive and never wore makeup. When the summer was over, she was going back to Yale University in Connecticut, where she was studying to become a photojournalist.

And then there was one-of-a-kind Emma Cresswell—undoubtedly the unlikeliest of all of them to end up taking care of kids for a family on Sunset Island. That's because Emma didn't have to work a day in her life if she didn't want to. Emma was the daughter of Katerina and Brent Cresswell, of the Boston Cresswells, one of the richest families on the planet. Petite and perfectly blond, Emma had been nicknamed the ice princess by Sam. That was only a joke, though, because Emma was much more than an heiress. In fact, her dream was to join the Peace Corps and also to study primates in Africa.

"You think the air-conditioning is working in here?" Sam yelled over the music, which had gotten even louder. She held up her hair and fanned the back of her neck. "I'm dying!"

"It's a zoo in here!" Carrie yelled. "You guys want to go down to the beach? It'll be cooler!"

Emma and Sam nodded agreement vigorously, and they quickly finished their sodas and paid their tab. They ducked out the front door of the Play Café, turned left, and started walking a few short blocks toward the beach.

"Jeez," Sam said, when they were finally outside in the cool Maine night air. "I know that place is always crowded, but tonight you couldn't wedge another body in there!"

Emma thought about the recent fire at a new club, Surf's Up, and she shivered. "It's dangerous, don't you think? What if a fire broke out?"

"Stampede," Sam replied.

They crossed the street and in a matter of moments were standing on the boardwalk that ran along the beach parallel to the ocean.

They all stood quietly, breathing in the glorious night ocean air, looking out over the beach, which in the daytime was packed almost as tightly as the Play Café but at night was practically deserted.

"I love it here," Emma said softly. "This place is paradise."

"Sure, you would think that," Sam teased her. "Now that Kurt is back."

Emma smiled. Kurt Ackerman was the first guy she had ever loved. He'd grown up on Sunset Island, and he and Emma had started going out at the beginning of the previous summer. But things had gotten too serious too fast and they'd broken up—they both had thought forever. Kurt was so upset over it that he'd left the home he loved. Recently he had returned, and he and Emma were seeing each other again. *We're taking it slowly,* Emma thought, *but I really believe we have a chance. . . .*

Carrie sighed and stared out at the

ocean. "When I look out there, I think about Billy."

"When you look anywhere you think about Billy," Sam said.

Billy Sampson, Carrie's boyfriend, was the lead singer of Flirting With Danger—or the Flirts, as everyone called them. His dad had been in a serious accident back in Seattle, and Billy had had to fly home to take care of his dad's business. The truly terrible thing was he didn't know when—or even if—he'd be back to Sunset Island.

"So, did you decide if you're definitely going to go visit him in Seattle?" Emma asked her.

"I'm going to talk to him tomorrow night," Carrie replied. "If he still doesn't know when he's coming back, I'm going there."

"To visit, I hope you mean," Sam said.

"I don't know what I mean," Carrie admitted. She pushed a strand of windblown hair out of her eyes and leaned over the railing. "I just . . . I don't know what to do without him!"

Emma looked at her with concern. "That doesn't even sound like you."

"I know," Carrie agreed. "I'm not doing great."

"But you're the one of us who always has it together!" Sam exclaimed.

"Oh, Sam, that isn't true," Carrie said. "I don't know why you think that."

"Because compared to me you're like, so . . . so normal!" Sam exclaimed.

Carrie laughed sadly. "The truth is, I'm in bad shape. I can't sleep. I'm eating too much junk food. I yelled at Chloe about some dumb little thing—"

"She'll get over it," Sam said. "She's a happy little kid."

"I don't know if *I'll* get over it," Carrie admitted. "I feel overwhelmed. Even Graham and Claudia are worried about me. They told me so this morning."

Graham and Claudia were Graham Perry Templeton—*the* Graham Perry Templeton, legendary rock star and world-famous celebrity—and his wife, Claudia. Carrie was the au pair for their kids, thirteen-year-old Ian and five-year-old

11

Chloe. At first it had been a little weird working for someone as famous as Graham, but now Carrie was practically part of the family.

"We're worried, too," Emma said gently. "But I don't think there's really much anyone can do."

"That's what's so unfair!" Carrie wailed. "It's not like Billy and I had a fight or anything. Everything was so great!"

"Stuff happens," Sam remarked philosophically. "I mean, it's terrible Billy's gone, but—"

"Have you heard from him recently?" Emma asked, interrupting Sam.

"Every single day," Carrie confirmed. "Either a letter or a phone call." She stopped talking for a moment as a group of nighttime bicyclists rode by, their tires clicking out a weird syncopation on the wooden slats of the boardwalk.

"So at least you know Billy is still crazed for you," Sam pointed out.

"That's for sure," Emma chimed in.

"I know he loves me," Carrie said softly. "I know he wants to be here . . ."

"I know how tough it is on you," Sam said, "but it's tough on the band, too."

"Don't you think I know that?" Carrie asked defensively. "The Flirts mean everything to Billy!"

"And to Pres," Sam reminded her.

Three years earlier, Billy and Pres had started the band, Flirting With Danger, together. They had developed quite a following on the East Coast and a major record label was interested in them. Sam, Emma, and their arch enemy, Diana De Witt, had been chosen as backup singer-dancers for the band, and they had all toured with rock superstar Johnny Angel earlier that summer. Then Diana had been forced out, and now their friend Erin Kane was the third backup singer.

"I know this is hard on Pres," Carrie acknowledged.

"It's hard on everyone in the Flirts," Sam said. "I mean, we're kind of spinning our wheels now, wouldn't you say?"

"It's only been a little while," Emma offered. "Billy will be back soon."

"Maybe," Sam said, noncommittally.

"It's awful for Carrie, I know, but we're missing gigs all over the place. Pres says it hurts our rep."

"There's nothing Billy can do!" Carrie said emotionally. "I mean, what's he supposed to—"

Sam shrugged. "I'm just telling you what Pres and I talked about," she said. "I wish Billy were here, too."

"Everyone does," Emma said, trying to placate her friends.

"It's been a long time since we've even rehearsed," Sam reminded them.

"How can you be worried about band practice?" Carrie said, her voice rising.

"Because this band is not some cute little diversion!" Sam exclaimed. "It's Pres's entire life. Which means that right now his entire life is on hold!"

"Billy is Pres's best friend," Carrie said. "Are you telling me that Pres blames Billy because he left?"

"No, of course not," Sam said. "But didn't you say that Billy's dad is out of intensive care now?"

"Sam," Emma said gently, putting her

14

hand on Sam's arm, "it's still really diffi-
cult for Carrie."

"I know it's tough! But doesn't Billy
have some kind of commitment here?"
Sam queried.

"What, you expect him to just leave his
family? When his dad can't make any
money? Is that what you want?" Carrie
demanded.

"All I'm saying is that the world has to
go on, doesn't it?" Sam replied, running
her fingers through her wild red hair.

"The band can wait awhile," Carrie
said.

"The band *has* waited awhile!" Sam
reminded her.

"Take it easy, Sam," Emma said. "It
hasn't even been that long yet."

"I don't want to take it easy!" Sam
exclaimed, irritably. "This really ticks me
off! I mean, you and Carrie haven't exactly shut down the perfume business
because Billy went back to Seattle!"

"That's not the same thing!" Carrie
remonstrated.

"Oh, yeah?" Sam said angrily. "It seems

to me that when it comes to carrying on a business that's important to you and Emma, it's pretty much business as usual. Billy or no Billy!"

"That is not fair," Carrie cried. "You are acting like a total bitch!"

"Carrie, come on, you don't mean that," Emma began

"Oh, yes I do," Carrie insisted. "I'm sick of being nice and understanding while Sam gets to be crazy!"

"Hey!" Sam objected.

"It's true," Carrie said bitterly. "You get away with things and we just chalk it up to crazy ol' Sam. Well, I'm not feeling very understanding right now—"

"And I'm not crazy!" Sam yelled. "I'm the one who is being a professional, while you only think of yourself! It's easy for you to be selfish about this, because you're not even part of the Flirts!"

"Please, stop it, you two," Emma said. "I can't believe you're fighting about this—"

"You amaze me!" Carrie exclaimed, ignoring Emma. "You were ready to quit the band because you thought you were going to be a famous dancer working with that guy X who was on the island! You just take whatever position is convenient for you!"

"That isn't true—" Sam said.

"Come on—" Emma said.

"It is true and I'm sick of being nice about it!" Carrie yelled.

Sam gave Carrie a cold, angry look. "I'm outta here. If I stay one more minute, I'm going to say something I might regret—although right now it would just feel great." She turned and headed back up the boardwalk.

Carrie looked at Emma. "I'm right, you know."

"Goody for you," Emma said, suddenly tired of the whole thing herself.

"What, are you on her side?" Carrie asked.

"I'm not on anyone's side!" Emma yelled in frustration. "But I think both of you are acting like two-year-olds!"

"Oh, who cares?" Carrie asked crossly. "I'm sick of being mature. I'm sick of everything!"

"I have a feeling you need some time alone," Emma said. She hoisted the strap of her purse over her shoulder. "I'll see you tomorrow."

"I'll be twenty pounds fatter by then," Carrie said, "because I plan to go buy a gallon of ice cream and eat the entire thing."

"Knock yourself out," Emma said, walking away.

"Don't try to stop me!" Carrie yelled after her.

"I wouldn't dream of it!" Emma called back. "But you'll be sorry."

"Guess what?" Carrie yelled. "I don't care!"

Well, that about sums it up, Emma thought, as she walked toward the Hewitts' car that she'd parked near the Play Café. *I don't feel like caring tonight, either. I've got my own problems to worry about. If those two want to act like idiots, let them!*

All three girls went back to the homes where they lived and worked, and for the first time since they'd become friends, they didn't want to even think about one another. They got ready for bed and, still angry, settled in for the night.

What they didn't know was that they were about to share something besides anger. Some say the dream world can be a real world of another time, another place. Sam, Emma, and Carrie were about to enter this other world—the world of the future, of what could be.

And once they got there, nothing would ever be quite the same again.

TWO

Carrie's Dream

"Say cheese, babe!"

Carrie sighed to herself and fought to refocus her lagging attention on the June 2004 copy of *Twenty-first Century* magazine she was leafing through.

"I said, 'Say cheese, babe!'" her boss, Flash Hathaway repeated jocularly. "And when the Flashman says 'Say cheese,' the Flashman's employee sez it back!"

Carrie looked up from the magazine and stared at her boss, whom she loathed with every fiber of her being. Of course, she couldn't tell him that. "I was trying to figure out how to compose the new ad to fit this magazine's format," she explained.

Flash leaned over Carrie's shoulder and leered at the photo of the bikini-clad model showing off the latest shampoo. "The Flashman could do some composin' with that babe, and I don't mean just beautiful music, if you catch my drift!"

Unfortunately I've been catching your loathsome drift for eleven years now, Carrie thought to herself, but she didn't say a word. Instead she looked back down at the copy of *Twenty-first Century* magazine again and tried to concentrate.

I can't believe that of all the people in the world who could be my boss, I have to have Flash Hathaway, she thought.

Carrie recalled how she'd first met Flash eleven years before, back when she was seventeen and working as an au pair her first summer for Graham and Claudia Templeton on Sunset Island. Flash was a sleazy fashion photographer back then, who'd convinced Carrie's then-best friend, Sam Bridges, to pose for some compromising pictures, which he'd exhibited at a private strip club. And then Flash had been picked to be the official photographer on the big East Coast tour of Carrie's old boyfriend's band, Flirting With Danger.

Billy Sampson. Carrie thought to herself, her heart skipping a beat. *I haven't thought about him all week. Well, that's progress. But it still feels like there's a hole in my heart. And it's been ten years since I've spent more than a couple of hours with him.* She sighed and gulped hard. *And after all this time, I still miss him. . . .*

Carrie pulled herself back to reality. She had a job to do. She was a junior photographer for the Spectra Advertising Agency in New York City, one of the real up-and-coming ad agencies in Manhattan.

She'd been lucky to find the job. There was a terrible economic crisis when she'd been looking for work, and employers, when they decided to actually hire new people, were signing them to long-term contracts to make sure they wouldn't pick up and leave once they'd been trained.

Carrie had been no exception. Spectra made her sign a five-year corporate contract. And she didn't mind that much.

She'd started out shooting photos for their environmental advocacy group accounts. Her work was enjoyable and her boss seemed pleased with her photos.

Then came the interoffice memo that changed everything. She'd read it so many times, it had been etched into her brain:

SPECTRA ADVERTISING AGENCY
555 MADISON AVENUE
NEW YORK CITY
INTEROFFICE MEMO

FROM: WILLIAM MCWILLIAMS, PRESIDENT, SPECTRA
TO: ALL SPECTRA EMPLOYEES
SUBJECT: OWNERSHIP CHANGE

All employees please be advised that as of noon today, the ownership of our agency will change hands. Our parent company, Farleigh, Inc., has sold our agency to a consortium of investors based in California. The new chief executive officer will be Mr. Frederick Krummer; the new chief operating officer will be the well-known fashion photographer and photojournalist Mr. Flash Hathaway.

It has been a pleasure working with you. This will be the last memo that you receive under my name as president. Good luck with the new organization.

Bill

"So, you gonna say cheese, babe, or what?" Flash repeated, edging his way into Carrie's tiny cubicle.

"Cheese," Carrie muttered, mustering as much enthusiasm as she could.

"Much better," Flash replied, pushing hair up over his growing bald spot. "Come on down to the conference room with me, there're some people here I really want you to meet."

Carrie got up and followed Flash down the hallway, wondering who it was that Flash wanted her to see. Right after the change in ownership at Spectra, the company's environmental advocacy accounts had dropped the agency, and these days Carrie was mostly taking pictures of models with great hair for overpriced shampoo ads.

They're probably some of the shampoo people, she figured to herself.

Flash held the door open to the conference room, and Carrie walked in. She unconsciously ran her fingers through her chopped hair.

Why did I cut it all off, anyway? Carrie asked herself. *I look horrible in short hair.* She looked down at her baggy black jeans and oversized black sweater and realized she'd had this particular sweater since her days as an au pair on Sunset Island. She pulled at a loose thread. *I really need some new clothes,* she thought with a sigh. *But inflation is so high I can barely afford to buy a T-shirt!*

Sitting in the conference room were four middle-aged men, all white and all in suits, white shirts, and ties. Spread out on the conference table were mockups of magazine advertisements which Carrie guessed had been put together by a division of her agency.

"Carrie," Flash said grandly, "this is the senior marketing staff of the USA Tobacco Company. They're a new client!"

Tobacco? Carrie thought. *Did he just say tobacco?*

"Hello," Carrie said nodding.

"Hi, Carrie," one of the men said. "We understand you're one of the best."

"Thanks," Carrie replied.

"You're the ace, Flash says," another of the men answered. "That's why we're counting on you to do a bang-up job for us!"

"Thanks," Carrie repeated. *Please, don't let this be what I think it is,* she thought with dread. *We're going to be doing advertisements about cigarettes? You've got to be kidding me!*

"USA Tobacco makes Prism cigarettes," Flash said proudly. "Great company. Great product. That's what you're gonna be shooting."

"And a whole lot of others," the youngest-looking man said proudly.

"We're looking to boost American sales," said another.

"It's tough," said a third, "now that smoking's banned everywhere indoors and the government's taxing the hell out of us."

"But we're counting on you," said the senior marketing person, a florrid-faced man with beady little eyes. "These ads are going to hook kids into smoking right from the beginning!"

All the people around the conference table, including Flash, nodded eagerly. Flash took a pack of Prism cigarettes out of his sportscoat pocket and lit one up. "Great smoke, guys," he told the executives. "Really killer!"

"I don't suppose you meant that as a joke?" Carrie asked before she could stop herself.

No one laughed.

Carrie looked at the conference table again, taking in the mock-up ads. And what she saw made her stomach sink somewhere down toward the basement of the office building and made her want to drop out of sight altogether.

Oh, no. These are all ads that target teenagers, she thought, looking at the glitzy, cartoony, very twenty-first century advertisements. *This is totally horrible! Smoking is the worst! I can't believe I have to do this. This goes against everything I believe in.*

"Uh," Carrie stammered, "are you sure that I'm the right person to do this?"

Flash laughed a hearty laugh. "She's such a kidder," he said a little too loudly. "She's my best. Trust me. Alden'll do a great job."

He looked at Carrie, and his gaze was pure steel. "Right, Alden?" he asked, and there was steel, too, behind the question.

Carrie considered what would happen if she answered, "Wrong, Flash." She'd lose her job. She'd be in breach of her contract, which said that if she didn't work for five years, she'd have to pay back all the money they were going to pay her, plus a massive penalty.

Plus, the American economy was barely sputtering along. She might never find another job again.

"Right, Flash," Carrie said, hating herself even as she said it.

"See, what did I tell ya?" Flash grinned

at the execs. "These ads are gonna put Prism cigarettes in the purses of teen girls everywhere. Alden's your girl, Spectra's your agency. We're gonna make beautiful dollars together. And that's a promise from me, Flash Hathaway."

Flash took a long drag off his cigarette and blew the smoke in Carrie's face.

After she got off work that night, Carrie took the subway to the Astor Place stop, and then walked down St. Mark's Place in the East Village. She was more depressed than she'd ever been in her entire life.

Me, Carrie Alden, shooting photographs of cigarettes for ads aimed at kids, she thought miserably as she walked. *Whatever happened to all my dreams? I'm turning twenty-nine years old in a couple of months!*

Carrie kept walking, heading for her apartment at 98 East 7th Street. Ten years before, she and Emma had been on the roof of the same building when Emma had been sent out to a modeling shoot and Carrie had gone along. Now, irony of ironies, Carrie was living in a fifth floor walk-up apartment there.

Clang! Clang! Clang! The bells of St. Stanislaus Church, across the street from her building, rang out that it was eight o'clock.

Carrie let herself in the front door of the building.

"When you pay your rent?" her landlady yelled from down the hall. She was a small, wiry woman who had immigrated from Serbia some years before.

I get paid tomorrow, Carrie thought quickly. "I'll come pay tomor—"

"You pay tonight!" her landlady yelled up the stairs. "You owe money! You owe money!"

"But I don't get paid until tomorrow!" Carrie yelled back.

"You late!" The landlady accused, jabbing a finger in Carrie's direction.

"It's only the second of June," Carrie pointed out. "And I promise I'll pay tomorrow!" She escaped into the hallway. *It's hard, living from paycheck to pay-*

check, she thought with exhaustion. *So many people are doing it these days. How did things get so bad?*

She remembered back to her days on Sunset Island, with her two best friends, Emma Cresswell and Sam Bridges. *We were all so full of hope back then,* she thought, unlocking her tiny mailbox to see what had come that day.

The mail was boring. Bills. A bill from the electric company, a bill from the cable television company—they were offering a hundred and fifty channels now, but Carrie still thought there was never anything decent to watch. A bill from the bank that was handling her student loan from Yale, where she'd graduated seven years before.

Carrie huffed up the five flights of stairs to her apartment. *I really need to exercise,* she thought. *I am totally out of shape.* Her cat, Billy, greeted her at the front door with a meow. Carrie glanced at the answering machine. One message.

Great! Carrie thought. *Maybe it's that guy I met in the park at lunch last week.*

He seemed really nice. He promised he'd call me.

She pressed "Play" on the machine. Everyone else was using electronic voice mail these days, but she preferred her antiquated machine.

It wasn't the guy she'd met. It was a woman.

"Miss Carrie Alden, this is Miss Davis at Con Edison. Please call me at the number on your bill regarding immediate payment. This is your disconnect notice. Thank you."

Carrie sighed and reset the machine. Then she threw herself down on her futon couch and stared at the ceiling.

"Billy," she said to her cat, "things have to change for me. Because right now, I have no life." But try as she might, Carrie couldn't think of how to change a single thing without making everything a whole lot worse.

THREE

Carrie's Dream Continues

I have to get out of Spectra, Carrie thought to herself for about the zillionth time. *I have to change my life.*

It was two weeks later, and she had just spent another totally horrid day at Spectra Advertising taking pictures for Prism cigarette advertisements. They featured cute, cool-looking guys walking straight past gorgeous smoke-free girls and stopping to light the cigarettes of much plainer girls who were holding out Prism cigarettes.

I hate myself for working on those ads, Carrie thought dismally as she let herself into her apartment.

Billy the cat rubbed up against her,

and she leaned over to scratch between his ears. "Well, Billy, it's just you and me as usual," she told him with a sigh. "But today maybe I really *am* going to change some things."

Carrie put on a comfortable old set of Yale University sweats, set up her laptop computer on the tiny table in her kitchenette, plugged the telephone cord into the back of the computer and, her hands shaking a little with anticipation, logged onto the new computer network she had read about the week before in the *Village Voice*, a popular local newspaper.

It said you could place personal ads by computer for free, Carrie recalled. So I logged on and left one. I mean, I haven't had a real date in about two years. And I haven't really been in love since Billy all those years ago.

Now, there I go again. Thinking about Billy Sampson. I have to stop that. Next thing, I'll be thinking about Emma and Sam, and I sure don't want to do that. I've barely spoken to the two of them since we had that horrible fight on Sunset

Island, Carrie thought. *Over what? Nothing! We got through that summer barely talking to each other again, then went our separate ways. And they were the best friends I ever had.*

Carrie forced the thoughts of her old friends from her mind and signed on to THE RELATIONSHIP CONNECTION. Not a computer "chat" line—she was way too shy for that—THE RELATIONSHIP CONNECTION was set up for adults to leave personal ads for each other. Carrie had thought long and hard before she'd composed her ad. Now, before she checked the network for replies, she reviewed the ad she'd placed.

Straight, single white female, twenty-eight years old, brown hair and eyes. Attractive, Yale-educated, into photography, books, and knowing about the world. Looking for a great guy who'll sweep me off my feet. Your mother will love me!—CARRIE

"Your mother will love me," Carrie read aloud with a groan. "Now why did I write that? I sound like an idiot, which means if I attract any guys they'll be the kind who are attracted to idiots."

She typed in the commands on the computer keyboard that led her to the reply section. She was half-expecting to see nothing. So when she saw the screen listing responses, she gasped.

There were fifty-five replies to her ad.

"Billy, what am I going to do?" she said. Having lived by herself for so long, she'd gotten into the habit of talking out loud to her cat.

"Meow," the cat replied.

"Thanks," Carrie said, laughing for the first time in ages. "I agree."

She started at the beginning, patiently reading responses, carefully noting the number of any response that interested her and quickly deleting any that were clearly wrong.

"Oh, Billy, listen to this one!" she exclaimed to her cat. "I have the face of a movie star and the body to go with it," she read out loud. "I look great in my underwear, but I'd look even better in yours."

She shuddered and scratched the cat behind his ears. "Billy, there are some truly sicko guys out there."

Reading through the replies took more than an hour and a half. Many of the ad responses just left a guy's name, a phone number, and an invitation to join him at his apartment for the evening if she felt like it. These Carrie deleted right away.

When she was finished there was one left out of the whole batch that seemed actually interesting. Carrie read it over again:

Carrie—
I love your name, ever since I read Theodore Dreiser's novel *Sister Carrie*. Of course, no one reads anything anymore—with all the interactive games and virtual reality toys, who bothers with books anymore, anyway? So it's okay if you haven't read this one. It's pretty old, in any case.

Carrie had read *Sister Carrie* when she was a student at Yale and loved it. She read on.

So, as you can probably tell, I like books. Also professional sports. Also brunettes who went to Yale. I graduated from an Ivy League school, too. Princeton. Maybe you've heard of it. I'm fairly tall and in fairly good shape, have red hair and blue eyes. You and I are about the same age. I am employed by one of the major publishing companies in Manhattan, and I work a lot.

Anyway, why don't you call me? I'm sure we'll have a lot to talk about. And maybe we'll even like each other.

Then the guy left his phone number and his name: Graham.

That's a coincidence, Carrie thought. *I used to work for Graham Perry. God, I haven't talked to Graham in years. Chloe must be in high school now! I wonder if Ian is still trying to live up to his dad's reputation as a superstar? Although I know Graham hasn't recorded anything in years.*

Carrie thought a long time before she picked up the phone and dialed Graham's number. But she did it. And she liked him on the phone. The two of them set a date to meet that weekend for dinner at a restaurant on East 22nd Street called Pesca.

When Carrie hung up, she breathed a sigh of relief. "Well, Billy," she told the cat, "I might not know who this guy Graham really is, but at least I have a date."

Billy's only response was to look at her with his big eyes as if she were abandoning him already.

"Okay, Carrie, you can do this," she told herself before she walked into the front door of Pesca the following Saturday night. She glanced down at the outfit she'd chosen—after trying on everything in her meager wardrobe. She had on a pair of navy blue silk pants with a matching silk shirt. *Truly ordinary,* she thought, as a blonde in the latest style—see-through pajamas over skimpy under-wear—sashayed by her. *Well, I wasn't the see-through-clothes type ten years ago, and I guess I haven't changed,* she thought. She ran her hand through her short hair and caught a glimpse of her reflection in the glass front of the restaurant. *Maybe the fresh-faced, no-makeup look doesn't work as well at twenty-eight as it did at eighteen,* she thought anxiously. *I am not a kid anymore.* Only that morning she had experienced the horror of discovering a gray hair.

She took a deep breath and pulled open the door to the restaurant. The first thing she thought was that her blind date had stood her up.

I know Graham said to meet him at the bar right inside the front door, Carrie recalled, looking around.

But as Carrie scanned the bar, there was no one sitting there who fit his description.

There was, in fact, only one guy in the

whole place. He was sitting by himself at the far end of the bar. He was short and chubby and wore the latest in trendy fashion for men: suspenders over an otherwise naked torso, and super baggy pants. He looked like he was in his forties. The hair he had left was a sort of pale red. *Oh no*, Carrie thought, *red hair. Could that actually be . . . ?*

The guy spotted Carrie, stood up—Carrie guessed he was barely five foot six inches tall—and walked toward her.

"Carrie Alden?" he asked, sticking out his hand.

For a second, Carrie thought about denying her own identity, saying that her name was Diana De Witt or Lorell Courtland, or any one else on the entire planet as long as it wasn't her. But she automatically smiled and stuck out her hand.

"That's me," Carrie said graciously.

"I'm Graham Parton," the guy said, grinning wildly. "It's nice to meet you. Isn't this exciting?"

"Very," Carrie said, waiting for Graham to let go of her hand, which he finally did.

"They're holding a table for us in the back," Graham said. "I eat here all the time."

"That's nice," Carrie said, not knowing what else to reply.

This is the same guy who answered my ad? she thought, as Graham led the way to the table. *He doesn't look like the description he gave at all. He's got to be at least twelve years older than me! He said he was attractive! He said he was in shape!*

They sat down. A waiter brought them wine, bread, and dinner salads. And Carrie and Graham had absolutely nothing to say to each other. Finally, Graham looked at Carrie and smiled.

"I'm not what you expected, huh?" he asked gently.

"You could say that," Carrie admitted. Even though she was loathe to hurt his feelings, she couldn't completely hide her irritation. "You didn't exactly tell me the truth about yourself, you know."

"I didn't lie," Graham said.

"You said you had red hair," Carrie said.

"I do," Graham answered. "Not much of it, but what there is is red."

"And you said you were tall," Carrie said, breaking off a piece of a roll and chewing on it thoughtfully.

"I am," Graham said. "Taller than you, anyway."

"I'm five five," Carrie said.

"See? I'm five six," Graham replied.

"And how old are you?" Carrie asked. "Really, how old are you?"

"About . . . thirty-five," Graham answered.

"What does that mean?" Carrie asked.

"Forty," Graham said reluctantly. "Okay, forty-two—but everyone tells me I look younger."

Carrie sighed. *Okay,* she said to herself. *At the very least, I should be able to get a decent dinner out of this. And okay, maybe he's not the right person for me. At least we can spend a pleasant hour together. Or something.*

"So what publishing company do you work for?" Carrie asked, politely making conversation.

"Do you want the polite answer or the honest answer?" Graham asked, taking a sip of red wine.

"Honest," Carrie replied.

"The honest answer is that while I usually tell people I work for one of the major book publishing houses, I don't."

"So in other words, you lied about that, too," Carrie said.

"Yeah," Graham said with a disarming grin. "The fact is that I work for *Skinny International*."

"You're kidding," Carrie replied.

"About *Skinny International* one does not kid," Graham answered.

Carrie recalled that *Skinny International* was a magazine that had started around the turn of the century. It featured articles about and photographs of extremely skinny models, both male and female, dressed in really, really skimpy clothes. Since about fifty percent of Americans had had the new surgery that gave them the wildly popular skinny look, *Skinny International* was hugely popular. Carrie thought that someday she'd see her former friend Sam modeling in it. But she never did.

"How'd you get the job?" Carrie asked.

"My father," Graham explained.

"He owns it?" Carrie asked.

Graham laughed. "Not quite. He's just the publisher."

"No offense, but aren't you bad for their image?"

Graham laughed. "Probably. But a guy built like me just makes all those surgically altered models feel superior—and everyone likes to feel superior." He took a sip of his water. "For example, you're enjoying feeling superior to me right now."

"No, I'm not," Carrie contended. "But I don't like being lied to."

"If I told you the truth, you wouldn't be here," Graham said. "And you'd never find out what a really nice guy I am."

Silence. Graham and Carrie had run out of things to talk about.

"So," Graham said quietly, "can I ask you a question?"

"Sure," Carrie replied unenthusiastically.

"When was the last time you were in love?"

"I don't want to talk about that," Carrie said quickly.

"Look, let's be honest here," Graham began.

"That's funny coming from you—"

Graham held up his hand to stop her. "Okay, I deserved that. It's pretty obvious you and I aren't going to set the world on fire—frankly, I prefer women a little more stylish than you, no offense— but maybe we can be friends."

"I don't think so," Carrie said bluntly.

Graham just raised his eyebrows. "Why, you have so many friends that you can't squeeze in another?"

I don't have any friends, Carrie admitted to herself, tears coming unbidden to her eyes.

"That's what I thought," Graham said, even though she hadn't answered him out loud. "Look, I was a jerk to lie to you, and I apologize. Now, how about a pal?"

Carrie managed a small smile. "That might be nice."

"Okay, so let's hear it," Graham said. "Who's the guy who caused you to run that ad?"

"How do you know there is one?"

"There's always one. When you're done, you can ask me about Sarah, if you want."

And suddenly Carrie found herself talking about Billy Sampson, even though she hadn't talked about him with anyone for years.

"He was the most wonderful guy," Carrie said quietly. "It was eleven years ago, and we met on Sunset Island in Maine. Those were the best two summers of my entire life. I had two best friends, Emma and Sam; we did everything together. And I couldn't believe Billy fell in love with me."

"Why's that?" Graham asked her.

"Because he was this big up-and-coming rock star, and I was your basic girl next door," Carrie answered, ignoring the plate of pasta that the waiter had just set in front of her.

"So you two were close?" Graham asked.

"So close," Carrie replied. "I loved him so much."

"So what happened?" Graham asked her, taking a bite of his pasta.

"He went back home to Seattle," Carrie answered, feeling a lump form in her throat.

"How come?" Graham asked.

"His family," Carrie replied softly, feeling the lump in her throat get larger and larger. "His dad had an accident, someone had to run the family business, and Billy went."

"Didn't you see him after that?" Graham asked.

"Well, yes," Carrie answered. "A couple of times. I went at Thanksgiving that first year, and he came to Yale to visit me, but . . ."

"But what?" Graham prompted her gently.

"But . . . that April I got a letter from

him. At Yale. He told me he'd fallen back in love with his high-school girlfriend."

"Ouch," Graham said wincing. "And—"

"And he married her six months later," Carrie sighed.

"Wow, that hurts."

"You want to know the worst part of it all?" Carrie asked plaintively. "He invited me to the wedding. Can you believe it? He invited me to his damn wedding!" Carrie took a sip of her water to try and compose herself. *After all these years, it still hurts so much. . . .*

"Where is he now?" Graham asked.

"I don't know and I don't care," Carrie said in a steely voice. But her shaking hands belied her words. "Ha. I'm as big a liar as you are," she finally admitted. "I've never gotten over him. And sometimes I think I never will."

FOUR

Carrie's Dream Goes On

"Yo, Alden," Flash called to her as he careened down the hall toward her cubicle Monday morning. "You finish the blowups for the new Prism ads yet?"

"I've got to develop the last roll I took on Friday," Carrie admitted, rubbing away the beginning of a headache with her fingers.

"Don't bother," Flash said, leaning on her cubicle wall. "I'm changing the whole concept. I think we've done enough with this whole doggie-looking-babe-with-a-cigarette-gets-the-cute-guy motif. I'm working on an entirely new concept."

"Swell," Carrie managed.

Flash narrowed his eyes. "Carrie, listen, you're not looking too great. You getting enough rest and exercise and all that?"

"Yes, I'm fine, thanks for your concern," Carrie answered automatically.

"Well then, you must not be getting enough of the old ba-da-boom!" Flash exclaimed, pumping his fist in the air lasciviously. He scrutinized her again. "You still got those Marilyn Monroe curves, but I gotta tell you, babe, you're looking a little worn around the edges. Kinda used up, if you catch my drift. It's not good for our image."

Carrie's head began to pound even harder. *Would a jury of my peers find me guilty if I just picked up the X-Acto knife and stuck it into his overfed belly?* she wondered idly.

"So, listen, here's the new concept," Flash continued, coming over to sit on the edge of her desk. He began to pick his teeth with a gold toothpick as he spoke. "We get a bunch of little girls—say, five, six years old, real cute—and we dress 'em up to look like they're, like, twenty-five, with sexy dresses and their moms' high heels, lots of makeup, that kind of thing. And each girl has a Prism cigarette poised between her fingers, trying to look tough. Now, is that concept killer or is that killer?"

"You're kidding?" Carrie managed to utter.

"Genius does not kid," Flash replied.

"But it's . . . it's despicable," Carrie cried.

"It's art!"

"It's disgusting," Carrie said, "and I won't do it!"

Flash got up from Carrie's desk. "Excuse me?" he asked, his hand ostentatiously cupped to his ear. "What did I just hear you say?"

"I won't do it!"

"I don't think you mean that," Flash decided. "So, you ready to start interviewing the nymphets?"

At that moment Carrie knew she couldn't take it, not for one more minute, not even if it meant being in debt for the rest of her life. "Read my lips, Flash," she told him. "You are a sleazy, lowlife disgusting excuse for a human being. I loathe you. I always have. And I quit." Carrie began to gather up her stuff.

"You'll be sorry!" Flash yelled. "Nobody quits on the Flashman! I'll have you in court so fast you won't know what hit you!"

Flash continued ranting, but Carrie just walked away, out of the office and then out of the building for the last time.

She had exactly seventy-three dollars left to her name.

"Hi, Billy," she said with exhaustion when she got home. She petted the cat and then threw herself down on the bed. Tears welled up in her eyes and ran down her cheeks and onto the bedspread. "Billy, I have totally messed up my life."

The phone rang, and she rolled over to pick it up.

"Hello?"

"Hi, it's your new buddy, Graham," came the voice through the phone. "I thought you'd be at work—I was expecting to talk to your machine."

"Oh, hi, Graham," Carrie replied. She was actually glad to hear a friendly voice. "I just quit my job."

Graham whistled into the phone. "Is that brave or dumb?"

"Both," Carrie replied wearily. "What's up?"

"I called to invite you to a ritzy cocktail party tonight," Graham explained. "My dad is giving it at the new World Hotel on Park Avenue. Lots of celebs will be there—it should be a hoot."

"Thanks, Graham," Carrie replied, "but I wouldn't be very good company."

"Oh, come on," Graham wheedled, "maybe it'll cheer you up. Besides, neither one of us is dating anyone. Maybe you'll meet the new love of your life there while I'm scoping out the woman of my dreams."

Carrie thought about it a moment. *If I stay home I will just cry and eat a gallon of ice cream,* she thought. *I might as well go.* "Okay," Carrie decided. "I'll go—

although I don't have anything very fancy to wear."

"Not to worry," Graham said, "just wear something classic. I'll meet you in the lobby of the World at, say, seven, okay?"

"Okay," Carrie agreed. "Thanks for thinking of me."

"Hey," Graham said easily, "what are friends for?"

At seven o'clock that evening, Carrie paced the lobby of the World Hotel and nervously checked out her outfit again. She wore a plain black linen dress with a black linen jacket. Every woman who passed by her was arrayed in brilliant color, as was the current style. Their skirts were so short that they usually wore matching panties to complement their outfits. Carrie's dress came to just below her knees.

Drab, she thought miserably. *I am hopelessly out of date and totally drab.* She pulled nervously at her jacket, and a button came off and rolled across the lobby.

Oh, no, Carrie thought, and ran after the button. It had rolled under a large beige velvet chair. She got down on her hands and knees and felt around under the chair.

"I'd know that oversized butt anywhere!" came a laughing female voice, full of malicious glee.

Carrie felt her heart constrict with dread. It sounded so much like a voice from her past. *But it can't be,* Carrie thought. *I have to be hallucinating. It can't possibly be—*

Carrie poked her head out from under the chair and looked up at a smiling, perfectly groomed, drop-dead gorgeous Diana De Witt.

Diana De Witt. She had been Carrie, Emma, and Sam's archenemy on Sunset Island. And now here she was ten years later, smiling down at Carrie while Carrie rooted around on all fours for her missing button.

"I lost a button," Carrie said, getting up and trying to smooth her hair down.

"You've lost part of your hem, too," Diana pointed out.

Carrie looked down, and sure enough she'd managed to snag her hem so that two inches now drooped halfway to her calf. She looked back at Diana. Diana had on a silver minidress with matching silver panties. The material was so sheer over her bosom that it showed a tiny silver bra shot through with royal blue and purple threads. It clearly cost a mint, and Diana looked like a million.

"Well, how funny to run into you after all these years," Diana said with amusement, looking Carrie over from head to toe. "You haven't changed a bit."

"Neither have you," Carrie uttered.

"So, what brings you to New York?" Diana asked.

"I live here," Carrie said. "I work for . . . that is, I used to work for an advertising agency as a photographer."

"Oh, that's right," Diana said, nodding. "You used to take some little photos back on Sunset Island, didn't you?"

"I took some great pictures back on

Sunset Island," Carrie said firmly. "I was planning to be a photojournalist—"

"Why, that's right!" Diana agreed. "Now, that is just too funny! Because I'm a photojournalist!"

"No—" Carrie began.

"Yes!" Diana insisted. "I just got back from South America, where I did an award-winning spread for *Universal Magazine*—maybe you saw it?"

"No, I didn't," Carrie managed.

"And I did a brilliant thing for *The New York Times* last month on cultural bias," Diana continued. "Isn't it funny that we went into the same field?"

"Hilarious," Carrie replied with a sinking heart.

"So, what kind of photos are you taking now?" Diana asked, shaking her perfect chestnut curls back over her perfectly aerobicized shoulders.

I've been doing cigarette ads marketed to kids! Carrie wanted to scream. *I hate my life and there is no justice in this entire world!* But she didn't say that. She just couldn't bring herself to give Diana that kind of satisfaction.

"I'm doing some . . . freelance work," Carrie managed lamely.

"Carrie, there you are!" Graham said, rushing over to her. He had on a tux without a shirt, and he had put temporary tattoos on his chest and belly. It was a current fad among college guys, but on chubby Graham it looked ridiculous.

"Your husband?" Diana asked with amusement.

"My friend," Carrie corrected, introducing them quickly.

Diana looked Graham up and down. "Not exactly Billy Sampson, huh?"

I can't believe she said that, Carrie thought. It felt as if a knife were cutting into her heart.

An unbelievably handsome guy in a perfect tux walked over to Diana and put his arm around her. "Ready, Di?" he asked her, nuzzling her neck.

"Sure," Diana said. "Well, you'll have to excuse me. I'm the guest of honor at a cocktail party—"

"You're Diana De Witt?" Graham asked, wide-eyed.

"Yes," Diana replied coolly. "And you're—?"

"Graham Parton," Graham said eagerly. "My father is the publisher of *Skinny*. Listen, I love your work, and I hope you're going to agree to take some photos for *Skinny*—"

"We'll see," Diana said smoothly. "Now, if you'll excuse me. Oh, nice to see you again, Carrie, dear," she added. Then Diana put her hand on her escort's muscled arm and walked away.

"Please, just kill me now," Carrie mumbled under her breath.

"You know her?" Graham asked with excitement. "She's the best young photojournalist in town!"

"*I'm* a photojournalist!" Carrie cried.

Graham looked confused. "I thought you took photos for some advertising agency."

"Never mind," Carrie said with a sigh.

She and Graham walked into the cocktail party. Graham excused himself to go talk to someone or other, and Carrie was glad she wouldn't be forced to make conversation. She got a glass of wine and sipped it, thinking that she couldn't possibly feel any worse. But there, across the room, was a sight that made her heart clutch in her chest.

Emma Cresswell and Sam Bridges. Together.

It was too late now to run away. They turned in her direction. Carrie was rooted to the spot. Emma and Sam saw her at the same time. They both did a double-take, making sure it was really her.

Tears came to Carrie's eyes. *God, I miss them so much,* she realized. *What was it we fought about all those years ago? And how did we let it come between us forever? Correction. How did I let it come between us? Because I can see that Sam and Emma are still friends.*

"Hi," Emma said, walking over to Carrie, Sam right next to her. "It really is you, isn't it?"

"Have I changed that much?" Carrie asked.

"No, no, you look great," Emma insisted, but Carrie could tell she was lying.

She took in Emma's outfit. Emma still looked perfect. She had on a long white dress slit up to the waist at the side. Carrie turned to Sam, who had on a pink-and-red minidress over pink-and-red panties. The dress was held up at the shoulders with tiny rhinestoned straps. Carrie looked down at Sam's feet, and there she saw red cowboy boots. Sam's trademark red cowboy boots. A lump the size of Manhattan filled Carrie's throat.

"How are you guys?" Carrie asked.

"Great!" Sam said. "I have ten of my own boutiques across Europe, and in six months I'm opening another one on Fifth Avenue!"

"That's wonderful," Carrie said warmly. "And you, Emma?"

"Well, after I spent those two years in Africa with the Peace Corps, I started a worldwide charity for children," Emma explained. "President Kennedy—well, I call him Joe—is awarding me a Medal of Freedom at the White House next month!"

"I'm happy for you both," Carrie said. *Please, just let me sink into the floor and fade away to nothing,* she thought to herself. She took a deep breath, searching for something to say. "Hey, you'll never guess who's here?" Carrie said, striving to put some animation in her voice. "None other than Diana De Witt!"

"We know," Emma replied, looking puzzled.

"You do?" Carrie asked.

Emma nodded. "Of course. She's here with us. The three of us share a huge penthouse apartment on the Upper East Side. Of course, we all travel so much that we're not there too often, but still, it's home."

Carrie looked at Sam. "You live with Diana De Witt?"

"She's terrific," Sam said. "She's an incredibly talented photojournalist. Say, didn't you used to want to do something or other with photography?"

"Uh, excuse me," Carrie said. "I . . . I have to go."

"Well, it was nice to see you again," Emma said politely.

Neither Emma nor Sam asked for her phone number. They didn't hug her. They didn't even sound particularly happy to have run into her. And they certainly didn't stop her from leaving now.

Carrie turned away, and with tears blinding her vision, she ran out of the hotel and into the night. She stared up at the starry sky, tears running down her face.

"If only this was a dream," she sobbed. "If only I could go back and do it all again!"

But the man in the moon just gave her a knowing smile and didn't say anything at all.

FIVE

Emma's Dream

Emma sighed and patted her lips with a pristine linen napkin, then she put it down on the hand-carved marble table in front of her, next to her half-eaten chicken salad. She looked at the ornate gold calendar on the Louis XIV table next to the couch. June, 2004, it read. *How can it possibly be the year 2004?* she thought to herself. *I remember ten years ago, when I was nineteen, thinking how old I would be at the turn of the century. I thought I'd be doing all these incredible things with my life, not living here in—*

Just then the doorbell rang, startling her out of her reverie. She glanced over at the living room clock. It was 1:15 in the afternoon, and she'd just finished the lunch the cook had prepared for her and left in the refrigerator.

Odd, she thought to herself, *I wasn't expecting anyone to be calling on us so early today.* She got up from the couch, where she'd been reading a copy of *Paris Match* magazine while she nibbled half-heartedly at her lunch, and walked to the door to see who was there.

It's so rare I ever answer the door, she realized. *Usually, one of the butlers gets it. But it's Byron's day off, and Chadbourne had a terrible toothache and had to go to an emergency dental appointment, so no one is here. Just my luck.*

She peered out through the peephole of the imposing front door of the suburban Boston mansion where she and her husband, Trent Hayden-Bishop III, had been living ever since they got married six years before, but couldn't see anything.

That's strange, Emma thought, as she squinted out. *Maybe I'm hearing things.*

Puzzled, she swung the door open.

Standing in front of her was a diminutive sandy-haired boy—he looked to Emma like he was all of eleven or twelve years old—dressed in a green shirt, green trousers, and even green sneakers. He was wearing a white political button with green lettering on it and carried a green shopping bag with white lettering.

The campaign button on the boy's shirt read, "I'M GREEN FOR KURT! ACKERMAN FOR CONGRESS."

"Hi!" the boy said eagerly. "My name is Carl Lowe. Are you a registered voter?"

Emma was caught between a strong urge to swing the door shut in the boy's face and a desire to not hurt the boy's feelings and encourage him to participate in the political process. And for a moment, Emma thought she could have been looking at Wills Hewitt, the cute kid she'd taken care of all those years ago on Sunset Island.

Kurt's running for Congress, she thought as the boy looked at her intently, waiting for her to answer his question. *I read about it in the newspaper, but I didn't actually think—*

"I said," the boy repeated, "are you a registered voter in Massachusetts?"

"Yes," Emma said, letting her desire not to hurt the boy's feelings win out. "I'm a registered voter here. It's every citizen's duty."

"Yes, ma'am," the boy agreed emphatically.

Did he just call me ma'am? Emma thought, startled. *Am I really old enough to be called ma'am?*

"I'm part of the Ack Attack!" the boy continued, his voice full of enthusiasm.

"Very nice," Emma managed to reply.

"He's the greatest!" the boy continued eagerly. "He's for the environment—that's why we're all wearing green—and he's against nuclear power, and for solar, and against overpopulation, and . . . well, it's all right here in this literature."

The boy thrust a piece of campaign literature at Emma, who took it and held it, not knowing what she should do next.

"Could you please look at it, ma'am?" the boy asked politely.

"Oh, yes," Emma agreed. She glanced

at the boy again. *He really does look so much like Wills Hewitt. But Wills must be a young man now, maybe in college, maybe even married. . . .*

"Are you okay, ma'am?" the boy asked Emma.

"Oh, I'm fine," Emma assured him. "You just look like someone I know. Someone I *used* to know," she amended.

She took a deep breath before she could face looking at the campaign literature, then she held it up. Her heart sank. The front of the pamphlet featured a huge photo of Kurt, dressed in jeans and a white tennis shirt, his shock of dirty blond hair windblown and gorgeous, looking just a few years older than the boy she had fallen in love with eleven years earlier. Looking not much different than the same boy she had almost married eleven years earlier that magical summer on Sunset Island.

Not able to help herself, Emma opened the pamphlet. She gasped. In the upper right-hand corner of the pamphlet was a photo of Kurt that she recognized.

God, she thought, with a shock of recognition, *that's the photo Carrie took of Kurt and me on the beach at Sunset Island during the first annual Sunset Island Couples Olympics. I've got a copy of it upstairs! But I can't believe it! They cropped me out of the picture so they could use it in this literature.*

"I've even met him!" the boy boasted, his voice pulling Emma away from her fixation on the photo. "I got to shake his hand at his headquarters."

"So did I," Emma murmured.

"You did?" the boy said, incredulous and impressed at the same time. "He shook your hand? Because Kurt doesn't much like rich—" The boy caught himself, and a red blush of embarrassment began to spread over his face from his neck to his forehead.

"You're right," Emma said, a bitter little smile playing over her lips, "Kurt never did like rich people. Not when I knew him, anyway."

"When did you know him?" the boy asked eagerly.

74

"It was a long, long time ago," Emma said sadly. She opened the accordioned pamphlet and felt herself turn pale. "No! It can't be!" she cried.

"Are you sure you're okay?" the boy asked, looking worried.

But Emma barely heard him. She was staring at yet another photo of Kurt, this time with his arm around a beautiful, immaculately groomed woman who Emma knew only too well.

It was Diana De Witt.

The caption under the photo read "Kurt Ackerman with his fiancée, Peace Corps Director Diana De Witt. Mr. Ackerman and Ms. De Witt will be married at a special ceremony at the United Nations in New York City in late June."

"Not Diana! Please, anyone but Diana!" Emma moaned.

The young boy touched her arm solicitously. "Hey, do you need me to get you a doctor or something, ma'am?"

"Stop calling me ma'am!" Emma snapped, and was then immediately appalled at her own lack of manners. "I'm sorry," she told him quickly. "It's just that . . . I know her." She pointed at Diana's photo, unable to utter her name out loud.

The boy gazed at the photo. "Isn't she beautiful?" he breathed. "Did you know she raised two million dollars for UNICEF last year?"

"No, I didn't," Emma managed.

"I have an autographed picture of her," the boy continued. "She made me give her a one-dollar donation for Save the Children to get it, but it was worth it. So, can I count on your vote for Kurt Ackerman, ma'am?"

Emma couldn't look at his eager, infatuated young face another moment. She did the rudest thing she had ever done in her entire life.

She swung the door shut in the boy's face.

Two hours later, Emma was up in her office, digging through a closet full of boxes of papers, looking for something. The office, which featured a spectacular view of the surrounding countryside, was furnished simply but elegantly with Finnish-designed furniture, a beige office chair, and a laptop computer. There was also a phone bank which Emma used to coordinate volunteers for the pedigreed dog and cat shows she helped run.

At the moment, though, Emma wasn't looking for information about a show. She was searching for something far more personal. And finally she found it.

I haven't looked at these in years, Emma thought. *When Trent and I got married, I promised myself I'd banish Kurt from my mind. I promised myself. Now, I'm breaking the promise I made. I hope I won't be sorry, but I know already I will be.*

She reached down and picked up a big stack of papers, letters, and a bound diary. She was certain it was her mind playing tricks on her, but they still seemed to smell of the Sunset Island beach and ocean breeze. And then, Emma caught a tiny whiff of Sunset Magic, the perfume that she and Carrie had created together during their second summer on the island, and which later evolved into a very successful business for them both.

And then, much later, a nightmare, Emma recalled. *But I won't think about that now.*

Emma picked up a beautiful tapestry-covered book.

That's the diary Aunt Liz gave me when I went to Sunset Island that first summer, Emma thought, a massive lump filling her throat. *God, I was so young and so hopeful then.*

Still sitting on the floor by the closet, Emma screwed up her courage and opened the diary. Her life from that time, years ago, coursed through her veins again as she flipped through the entries. Finally, she came to one that made her stop and read the whole thing.

Dear Diary,

Sam, Carrie and I had the worst fight tonight. It was a nightmare. Sam got so angry at Carrie, and Carrie got just as angry at Sam. Sam was talking about how the band should go on without Billy being there, and Carrie got mad at her. Then Sam got mad at Carrie because we were still working on the perfume even though Billy was gone! And I was caught right in the middle—both of them got mad at me, and I didn't even do anything. I didn't know what to do, really.

Everything is a mess. Sly is probably going to die of AIDS, and Billy may never come back to the island. I feel like Carrie, Sam and I are growing apart. Maybe we never really did have all that much in common. Sam is so flighty, and these days Carrie is so depressed about Billy having to go home to Seattle that she can't think about anything else. Maybe I should just be concentrating on trying to mend my relationship with Kurt. Right now Carrie and Sam both just seem like infants, and I don't have the energy to spend while they try to figure out their problems. I'm going to sleep.

That was the beginning of the end, Emma thought sadly, as she finished the diary entry. *It all started to fall apart for the three of us that night.*

She leafed through later diary entries of that same summer, the last summer that she'd spent on Sunset Island, stopping to read a few all the way through.

Dear Diary,

I can't believe what's happening with everything. It's been a week and we're still not talking to each other. Well, Sam called me once, and Carrie called me once, but Sam and Carrie haven't said a word to each other since that night. Even Kurt's trying to patch things up, but he isn't having any luck.

Emma leafed through the diary some more. *Oh yes,* she thought, as she came to a particular entry. *I remember this night*

*really, really well. Everything should have
been fine from that night on. But it wasn't.*

Dear Diary,

Billy's back! He got back from Seattle
today. Everything's fine at his house—
his father's injuries aren't as bad as
the doctors thought at first, and he's
going back to work in a couple of days.
We all went out for dinner tonight to
the Sunset Inn: Kurt and I, Billy and
Carrie, Pres and Sam. The guys all get
along great. But between me and Carrie and Sam, it's as if someone put up
walls. I just don't understand it and I
feel as if it's my fault. Is it? Is there
something I should be doing that I'm
not doing?

And that was that, Emma remembered. *Oh, we'd see each other now and
then, and we even sang together in the
Flirts for a while. But then Sam quit the
band to concentrate on designing clothes,
and then I quit the band because the*

*perfume business was getting so success-
ful, and then* . . .

Emma closed the diary and put it down.
There were a few tears in her eyes, and
one of them dropped onto the diary's cover.
She picked up a stack of old Christmas
cards that were in the same box. Cards
from Carrie and Sam. They'd come for
a few Christmases after they'd all left
the island, but then they stopped—*right
around the turn of the century,* Emma
remembered.

Under the last Christmas card was a
letter in an envelope postmarked Sunset
Island, Maine. It was from Kurt, and had
arrived two years before she and Trent
were married. Emma hadn't looked at it
since the day before her wedding. But
now she took the letter up in her hands
and began to read it again.

Dear Emma,

Thought you'd never hear from me
again, huh? Surprise. It wasn't easy to
track you down, but I made some in-

quiries on the Internet, and they led me to you. I know you still think that when I broke up with you it was because of your money, but it wasn't. I guess I'll never get you to understand. We were just too different, Emma. We wanted different things. I'm dedicating my life to making this world a better place, and I need a partner who cares about that as deeply as I do.

Once, a long time ago, when you broke up with me, you told me you hoped we could still be friends. Well, I couldn't understand that at the time, but now I can. I hope we can be friends, Emma. Because we're going to be neighbors. At least, in the same state. I'm coming to Massachusetts, too, now that I'm done with my stint in the Peace Corps. It was amazing in Africa, and I'll have to tell you about it sometime. I never blamed you for leaving Africa after two weeks, Emma. I guess you were never really cut out for the Peace Corps.

There's no shame in that. You just weren't raised for that kind of life.

Remember I always told you I wanted to end up in politics. And I'm going to do it, too. This country's in big trouble, and somebody has to step forward. It may as well be *me*.

I hope you write to me. Here's the address.

Emma stopped reading.

I never did write to him, she thought. *Am I the biggest fool in the world? I loved him, and he loved me. I loved him more than I've ever loved anyone in the world.*

"And he actually ended up with Diana!" Emma cried out loud. "How? How could it have happened?"

Just then the phone rang. Emma guiltily shoved the papers and diary back into the box they'd come from, even though no one would ever dare come into her office unannounced, not even her husband. Then she reached for the phone and answered it in her usual proper tone of voice.

"Hello, Emma Hayden-Bishop speaking," she said, still wondering whatever possessed her to take the name of her husband when they'd gotten married. *I liked Cresswell,* she thought to herself. *And I don't like Hayden-Bishop. It's stupid and pretentious. Just like my life.*

"Oh, Emma," a familiar voice cried, "it's so lovely to speak to you. I've simply been dying to!"

Emma frowned. It was Carla McGovern, a woman about her age whom Emma had met at one of the cat shows she'd organized. Carla had immediately decided that Emma was going to be her best friend. For the rest of both their lives. Unfortunately, Emma didn't feel the same way about Carla. In fact, she found Carla to be a crashing bore.

"Oh, hello, Carla," Emma said, her voice tired and flat.

"Emma, are you okay?" Carla asked.

"Fine," Emma replied.

"Because, you know, if anything is

wrong, you can always call Carla! You know I would never breathe a word of anything you ever told me in confidence to another living soul—well, not unless it was really juicy, that is!" Carla laughed as if she had just cracked the greatest joke in the history of the planet.

God help me, Emma thought as she struggled to think of something to say to this woman she didn't even like. *This is the best I can do for a friend? Why did I let things go with Sam and Carrie? Why did I let it all fall to pieces? How could I have been so incredibly stupid?*

"By the by, Emma, I ran into your mother over at the advanced aerobics class at the club this afternoon—she's looking marvelous."

"Mmmm," Emma murmured noncommittally.

"She looks as if she had another little nippy and tucky," Carla informed Emma. "But I guess you'd know, seeing as you live right next door to her!"

"Yes," Emma replied.

"Yes, she had some touch-up work done

again, or yes, you live next door?" Carla asked craftily.

"Yes, I live next door," Emma said, switching the phone to her other hand.

"Well, aren't you the sweetest of daughters, keeping your mummie's secret," Carla purred. "Listen, I hardly blame her for wanting to do upkeep. I mean, how else can she hope to hold on to her latest hubbie, and he is a devastating hunk of stud-meat, I might add. All of twenty-five, isn't he? Is he hubbie number six or number seven?"

"Carla, I was just about to go out—" Emma fibbed.

"Oh, so sorry!" Carla cried. "Here I am prattling on like we're two teenagers with all the time in the world. Well, I'll just give you a ringy-dingy later, sweetie. Bye!"

Emma hung up and put her head down on her desk in exhausted defeat. "I hate my life," she admitted out loud. She looked over at a photo on the rug that had somehow not gotten packed up with the others; a photo of herself, Carrie and

Sam on the beach at Sunset Island, ten years ago. Their arms were around each other, and they were laughing into the camera.

And the photo was already fading around the edges.

SIX

Emma's Dream Continues

"Emma, darling, I'm home!" Trent called as he marched into the library.

Emma was sitting on the couch, staring out the window. "Hello," she said dully.

Trent didn't notice. He kissed her cheek perfunctorily and headed for the bar, where he made himself a martini. "Mmmm, nectar of the gods," he said with satisfaction, taking his first sip.

"Perhaps you could limit yourself to one of those," Emma suggested. "We're having dinner with my mother and Rex."

"Darling, both your mother and her latest husband can drink me under the table," Trent said, loosening his tie.

"If you mean that they can hold their liquor and you can't, that is quite correct," Emma said stiffly.

Trent threw back the rest of his martini and immediately began to make another. "Emma, you've turned into such a prig," he chided her.

Emma stared at Trent's belly, which hung over his belt by a good three inches, even if it was swathed in the very best hand-sewn shirt from England. His cheeks were florid and red veins stood out around his nose. "You're an alcoholic," Emma said distinctly.

"And you are a bore," Trent said, dropping an olive into his drink. "Don't you want to hear about the stock market today?"

"No," Emma said. "What difference could it possibly make? We have more money than we could ever spend."

"You've never understood that money is an end unto itself," Trent said with satisfaction, taking a deep guzzle of his second martini. He came to sit on the chair across from her and put his feet up on an embroidered footstool. "Oh, I've got news. We've got an invitation that I think will amuse you. Saturday night we're invited to a thousand-dollar-a-plate fundraiser for an old flame of yours."

Emma's heart lurched in her chest. "Really?"

Trent nodded. "None other than Kurt 'Aquaman' Ackerman," he said with relish, taking another guzzle of his martini. "The poor, dumb jock you once lusted after, all those years ago."

"I didn't lust after him," Emma corrected. "I loved him. And he's not dumb."

"Please," Trent scoffed. "He hasn't got two cents to rub together."

"What does that have to do with brains?" Emma asked with exasperation.

"Really, Emma," Trent said, "you are too, too droll." He got up to make himself a third drink.

"Well, I know you're lying about being invited to some kind of fund-raiser for him," Emma said primly, her hands folded in her lap. "First of all, Kurt is a Democrat, and you are a conservative Republican. And second of all, he would never permit a thousand-dollar-a-plate fundraiser. It goes against all his principles."

"Dear Emma. You are too old to be so naive," Trent informed her, his voice dripping patronization. "We give to both parties, so that we have influence with whomever might win. And the dinner is being done under the guise of a fundraiser for the Peace Corps, in honor of Kurt's lovely fiancée."

"Diana De Witt," Emma murmured.

"Oh, so you've heard," Trent said. "And here I thought I was going to have the pleasure of informing you."

"I just can't believe it," Emma said in a choked voice.

"Believe it," Trent said, his voice beginning to take on the harsh edge it got when he'd been drinking. He narrowed his eyes at Emma. "To think that Aquaman ended up with Diana, and I ended up with you."

Emma held her head high. "What's that supposed to mean?"

"It means that Diana is everything a

man could ever want in a woman—
gorgeous, passionate, smart, savvy—
while you . . ."

"What?" Emma snapped. "Go ahead
and say it."

"While you give new meaning to the
word, 'cold fish,'" Trent pronounced. He
began his third drink.

"And just how would you know how
passionate Diana De Witt is?" Emma
asked sharply.

Trent looked at her over the rim of his
martini glass. "You figure it out," he said
smugly.

Emma got up from the couch. "You
slept with her?"

Trent grinned maliciously. "I wouldn't
exactly put it in the past tense, dear."

Emma's hands flew to her chest. "You're
having an affair with Diana De Witt?"

Trent didn't say a word; he just continued to grin and sip his drink.

"Why did you ever marry me?" Emma
asked him.

"A question I often ask myself," Trent
replied. "You were such a wreck after

Kurt dropped you. And you made such a failure of that silly little Peace Corps venture—"

"It was what I had always dreamed of doing," Emma recalled sadly.

"Well, they sent you packing after two weeks, didn't they?" Trent reminded her. "You were upset because there wasn't anyplace to plug in your hair dryer, as I recall—"

"No, no, that's not the kind of person I am—"

"Oh, yes, it is," Trent said. "You always wanted to think you were different, but the truth of the matter is, you're just like your mother." He took another sip of his drink. "And that," he concluded, "is exactly why I married you."

"But I don't even like you," Emma whispered.

Trent laughed merrily. "I don't like you, either, dear! But we are ever so appropriate for each other, don't you think? And we are certainly going to this dinner for Aquaman on Saturday. Try to look your best." He scrutinized her from head to foot. "It might be time for your first little face-lift, Emma."

"But I'm not even thirty years old!" Emma protested.

Trent sipped his drink. "Passionless women age quickly, my dear. They age very, very quickly indeed."

Rexy want another oyster?" Emma's mother, Kat Strommer (formerly Cresswell, and then five other last names), asked her twenty-five-year-old husband in baby talk.

"Sure," Rex said, opening his mouth.

Kat forked a raw oyster into Rex's mouth, then kissed him. "There, sealed with a kiss," she said girlishly.

I want to throw up, Emma thought to herself. *My mother is almost sixty years old. Baby talk does not cut it.*

"Emma, aren't you enjoying your sole?" Kat asked her daughter with concern.

"Oh, it's fine, Mother," Emma said, forcing herself to fork a small piece of fish into her mouth.

"So, how are your little dog and cat shows going?" Kat asked her daughter.

"Fine," Emma said dully. "I'm planning a new show at Madison Square Garden in the fall."

Kat laughed her trilling laugh and took a sip of wine. "Oh, Lord, Emma, do you remember when you used to be obsessed with monkeys?"

"Not monkeys, Mother," Emma corrected her. "Primates."

"Same thing!" Kat said, laughing gaily. She leaned over and squeezed Rex's bulging bicep. "You wouldn't believe it, darling. Emma had a thing for monkeys! I'm so glad she switched to dogs and cats!"

"Monkeys, huh?" Rex asked.

Emma looked distastefully over at the young man who was her latest stepfather. Rex Strommer was six foot two, with perfect golden hair and bulging biceps. *And he has the brain of a turnip,* Emma thought to herself.

She remembered sadly that there was a time when she thought her divorced parents might get back together again.

They were seeing each other, and I was so hopeful, Emma recalled. *But then Dad had a second heart attack and died. And Mother has been in search of the fountain of youth ever since. She marries a younger guy every time, and he gets a big pile of her money in the divorce settlement.*

"Oh, Emma!" Kat cried gaily. "I forgot to tell you! There's going to be a mother-daughter luncheon at the club! Say you'll go with me!"

"I'm too busy," Emma said.

"Too busy for me?" Kat pouted at her daughter like a five-year-old. "I could ask Pierre to send us two darling originals from Paris—something that would match—wouldn't that be fun?"

"No," Emma said flatly.

"Oh, come on," Kat wheedled. "You know everyone says we look like sisters. We'll look so cute in little matching dresses, don't you think so, Rex?"

"Sure," Rex agreed amiably.

"Absolutely," Trent slurred, when he could manage to lift his lips from his martini glass.

"Mother, how could we look like sisters?" Emma asked in a steely voice. "You are almost sixty years old."

Kat sighed deeply. "You still get such joy out of humiliating me," she said in her most hurt tone of voice. "And I'm fifty-one."

"Whatever you say, Mother," Emma agreed.

Kat pouted and held her arms out to Rex. "Rexy, she's being mean to me!" she whined in a baby voice.

"There, there, now," Rex said, taking Kat in his arms. "Rexy will take care of you."

Kat snuggled up to her new husband. "Let's take a room here," she whispered, but was still loud enough for Emma to hear. Trent was too busy getting drunk to pay any attention. "I can't wait until we get back home, can you?"

"Uh-uh," Rex agreed. "Want to do it on the table?"

Kat giggled girlishly. "Oh Rexy, do get the check!"

Rex kissed his bride and excused himself.

Emma felt her stomach turn over. "Mother, you're disgusting."

"Emma, dear, I'm a woman," Kat said, her voice instantly going hard. "Which is certainly more than anyone can say for you."

"I'll drink to that," Trent agreed. And then he did.

Two hours later, Emma tiptoed past Trent, who was passed out and snoring loudly, and she made her way back into her office, where she took out her diary yet again. She picked up a pen and curled up on the couch.

Maybe if I write out how I feel, it'll make me feel better, she thought. *That used to help me so much. Maybe it's not too late. . . .*

Dear Diary [she wrote—and even though she felt stupid, she forced herself to continue],

99

I hate my life. I don't know how this happened. I turned into exactly the kind of person I have loathed my entire life. How, how could it have happened? Sometimes I wonder, if I had stayed friends with Sam and Carrie, would everything have turned out differently? Can friendship really have that kind of power? How could I have let all my dreams just slip away?

When I married Trent, I thought it would be safe, and I craved safety after Kurt dumped me. Now I see how utterly stupid that was. I truly cannot stand him, but maybe he's all that I deserve. I thought I was better than my mother, different, but now I see that I'm not. The joke is on me.

I wonder whatever became of Sam and Carrie. I haven't heard from either of them in years. Did their dreams come true?

Some mornings I wake up and think: today I will make a move, today I'll change things. But I never do. I am a boring, spoiled rich girl who plans ridiculous shows for pedigreed, pampered pets. I wonder, dear diary, at the ripe old age of almost thirty, is it still possible to change my life?

I would give anything to go back and do it again differently. Anything.

Emma.

SEVEN

Emma's Dream Goes On

"Oh, Emma!" a well-preserved woman in her fifties called to Emma from across the crowded ballroom. "Aren't you looking delicious!" She kissed the air near both of Emma's cheeks.

"Hello, Geraldine," Emma said politely. Geraldine Reynolds was one of her mother's friends, and Emma couldn't stand her.

"Your dress is just perfect," Geraldine insisted, taking in Emma's flowing column of sleek white silk. "From the La Scala Collection, isn't it?"

No, I got it at K Mart, Emma longed to say. But she didn't. "Yes, it is," Emma admitted.

"Well, it's perfect on you, darling," Geraldine said. "I'm just pea-green jealous. You must be a size three!"

"Five," Emma corrected the woman.

"We must shop together sometime," Geraldine insisted. "I do occasionally buy off the rack—it's so amusing when one actually finds something ready-made, don't you think?"

"Yes, it makes me laugh my head off," Emma agreed solemnly.

Geraldine's fixed smile didn't slip, though it was obvious she suspected Emma was making fun of her. "Well, I must run. Regards to your marvelous mother," Geraldine said gaily.

"You could have been nicer," Trent said. "Her husband is very influential."

"I don't really care," Emma told her husband. "I don't even want to be here."

Trent stuck his finger into the too-tight collar of his tuxedo shirt. "This damn shirt shrunk," he grumbled.

"It's brand new, that's impossible," Emma pointed out. "Maybe your neck just got fatter."

"Hello, Emma!" another friend of Kat's called, rushing past in a designer chiffon number. "Hello, Trent!"

"Oh, Emma darling, you look simply ravishing tonight," yet another matronly woman about her mother's age called to her. "Absolutely ravishing. Doesn't she, Clarissa? I love that dress!"

"Why, of course, Hildy," the woman sitting next to her said. "Such a Hayden-Bishop! And you look marvelous, too, Trent!"

"Thank you, Clarissa," Trent said, kissing the woman's hand. "You are a vision, I must say."

"I'd better be," Clarissa said, straightening the narrow strap of her emerald-green sheath. "I just spent two weeks at the Golden Palace Spa at Lake Geneva. It was absolutely brutal—but worth it."

"Oh, excuse us," Trent told her, "I see my business partner across the room."

Trent and Emma hurried off.

"I didn't know William was here," Emma remarked.

"He isn't," Trent admitted. "I just cannot stand that skinny old broad Clarissa Wesley. I don't care if she is richer than God—she's older than him, too. Let's go find our table."

Others greeted Emma and Trent as they threaded their way through the crowded ballroom at the downtown Boston Ritz-Carlton hotel. Many of Trent's business associates from his investment-advising business were at the Ackerman-for-Congress fund-raiser as well, and Trent nodded hello to some of them as they passed.

Hypocrites, Emma thought to herself as she passed them. *They're Republicans just like Trent. They're only here to try to peddle a little influence if Kurt happens to be elected. It's disgusting. I can't believe Kurt would let that happen.*

Trent led the way to a lavishly set table near the front of the ballroom and found the name cards marked for himself and Emma. Emma didn't recognize anyone else at the table, though Trent said hello to a few and introduced her as his wife. Then, as she sat down, Emma saw, not more than twenty feet away on the ballroom stage, a long, table with about fifteen empty seats behind it.

It must be reserved for Kurt and other dignitaries, she thought to herself. *He'll be up there with Diana. Oh, God, how will I endure it? He'll be able to see me from there easily!*

But even as red-tuxedoed waiters circulated around the room, serving shrimp cocktails to the guests, the head table remained empty.

Odd, Emma thought. *I wonder where they all are, and when they'll arrive.* She sipped at her water nervously. *I wish I were anywhere else but here right now.*

Suddenly, the lights in the room dimmed, and a spotlight burst on, shining directly on an enormous American flag hanging from the ceiling. Emma could see that it was a new flag—one that actually had fifty-two stars on it, since Puerto Rico and El Salvador had recently become states.

"Ladies and gentleman," a male voice boomed over a hidden sound system, "please rise for our national anthem!"

The crowd rose to its feet, and some people put their hands over their hearts, as the unaccompanied voice began to sing "The Star Spangled Banner":

O say! can you see by the dawn's early
  light,
What so proudly we hail'd at the
  twilight's last gleaming?
Whose broad stripes and bright
  stars . . .

That voice just sounds so familiar, Emma thought to herself. *I'm sure I know it— I've heard it on the radio, I'm sure I have!*

Just at that moment, another spotlight burst on, this time aimed at the right side of the head table. The person singing the national anthem was completely illuminated, and the crowd roared with surprise and delight.

It was the person whose song "The Haunted Heart" was currently at the top of both the adult contemporary and rock charts in *Billboard* magazine, and whose picture had recently been on the cover of *Newsweek, Time,* and *Twenty-first Century Magazine,* all in the same week.

Ian Templeton.

Emma gasped as Ian's blond-haired head was illuminated. Like the rest of the country, she'd been reading about Ian's exploits in the newspaper and heard all of his songs on the radio—they were inescapable. But this was the first time she'd seen Ian in the flesh since ten years before, on Sunset Island, when he was a not-quite-fourteen-year-old kid with an industrial-music band that made a rather dubious form of music.

Now look at him, Emma thought, as Ian soared through the song. *He doesn't look like a child anymore. Actually, he looks just like Graham, his father!*

Ian was dressed in a luxurious Italian tuxedo, a white shirt without a tie, and red shoes. His blond hair cascaded down past his shoulders. And he had the same angular features as his rock-star dad.

I wonder how Graham and Claudia are, Emma thought as Ian brought the song to a close. *They must be so proud of Ian. When Carrie was their au pair, they were always so nice to me. Now, I haven't seen them in so long, they probably wouldn't even know who I am.*

O'er the land of the free
and the home of the brave.

The well-mannered crowd applauded enthusiastically. The air was charged with electricity—they had just watched Ian Templeton perform! Ian was as famous as Michael Jackson or Garth Brooks had been more than a decade before.

"Thanks," Ian said easily as he accepted the ovation and cheers. "It's a pleasure to be here tonight. It's an honor to do my good friend Kurt the service of singing for him. We've known each other for years. He was nice to me when I was just a skinny little kid back at a place called Sunset Island."

I was there, too, Emma thought. *I was happy, then! Oh, how did it all go so wrong? How?*

At that moment Ian's gaze brushed across Emma's face. Emma felt a cold sweat break out on her neck.

I was always nice to him, too, Emma thought to herself as she felt Ian's quick cool stare.

But then another voice inside her said: "Yes, that may be true, but you and Sam and Carrie used to poke fun at his band behind his back. Sometimes in public. That had to get back to him. That had to hurt. Didn't you think you might be hurting his feelings? Didn't you care? Maybe you were really totally self-involved back then, and the life you have now is all that you deserve. . . ."

Ian shifted his gaze back to the crowd. "Remember, Kurt will be nice to *you,* too, if you elect him. So do it!" he shouted good-naturedly. The crowd laughed and applauded again.

"Remember what a little jerk that kid was back on Sunset Island?" Trent asked in Emma's ear.

"He wasn't a jerk," Emma said sharply. "He was a very nice kid."

"Right," Trent said sarcastically. "I was on the island a few times. I remember how it was. The kid was a geek loser!"

"Well, he certainly isn't anymore, is he?" Emma pointed out coldly.

"Nope," Trent agreed. He reached for his third martini. "Who would have guessed!" He put his arm lightly around Emma's shoulders and looked around the ballroom. "Well, all the liberals are out in force. Let's just hope Ackerman doesn't actually get elected. What a zoo that would be!"

"Trent!" a middle-aged man called as he walked by their table. "Good to see you!"

"Hey, great to see you, Martin!" Trent

called back, a big grin on his face. "What an imbecile," Trent told Emma, the false grin still stretched across his lips. "He lost ten million in the market last week." Trent looked around and spied a waitress wearing a nametag that read JUNE. "Oh, June-y!" he yelled. "Bring me another mar-tooni! Ha! That's a little joke!"

Emma closed her eyes. It was going to be a very long night.

". . . and in conclusion," Kurt said boldly into the microphone, "let me repeat the words of John Kennedy from so many years ago: 'Ask not what your country can do for you; ask what you can do for your country!' Thank you all so much for being here. Thank you!"

The ovation that greeted the end of Kurt's stump speech was deafening.

"Jeez, can you believe these idiots lapping up this liberal crap?" Trent slurred in Emma's ear even as he was applauding along with everyone else.

"I happen to agree with everything Kurt said," Emma replied.

An aide whispered in Kurt's ear, and he leaped back to the microphone.

"One more thing!" Kurt said, a broad grin spreading over his face. "I want to give all my friends in the press the photo op they're begging for." Kurt turned to Diana De Witt, who was sitting a few seats to his left. She looked absolutely ravishing in a black lace strapless dress that enhanced her perfectly aerobicized curves. Kurt held out his hand, and Diana stood up.

"She looks good enough to eat," Trent said sloppily.

"Shut up," Emma snapped.

"If you can't take the heat, my dear, get out of the kitchen," Trent told her.

As Emma watched wretchedly, Diana got up, walked over to Kurt, waved to the crowd, and took Kurt's hand.

"My lovely fianceé, Ms. Diana De Witt!" Kurt called into the microphone.

The audience applauded even more enthusiastically, and Kurt leaned down and kissed Diana on the lips. "Is she the greatest, or what?" Kurt asked the crowd. "She's gonna make 'em forget all about Hillary Clinton and Tipper Gore! Now, Diana and I want you all to have a terrific time at the party!"

As Kurt uttered these last words, a huge curtain at one side of the ballroom was drawn open, revealing another room as large as the ballroom they were now in. It was decorated with hundreds of big United Nations flags and hundreds of "Green for Kurt: Ackerman for Congress!" green placards, and banners proclaiming "Have an Ack Attack!"

"Can we go now?" Emma asked Trent, as everyone in the ballroom stood up and started to make their way into the party room.

"Emma, you are just so amusing," Trent answered her lightly, taking a sip from yet another martini. "Of course we can't leave."

"Why not?"

"Business, Emma dear," Trent said in the same light tone of voice. "It's business.

The business of politics!" Trent laughed at his own lame joke. Then he took Emma by the hand and practically dragged her into the party room.

There was a dance combo playing, and still more waiters and waitresses were circulating, this time with all kinds of fingerfoods and desserts on their trays.

"Emma?" a female voice asked from behind her. "Emma Cresswell?"

Emma turned, but all she could see was an attractive, slender young brunette woman with a short, very chic haircut. The woman had about five cameras slung over her perfectly tailored gray flannel jacket. Emma could see that she was carrying press credentials from *The New York Times*.

"Do I know you?" Emma asked.

"Emma," the woman said, "I'm Carrie. Carrie Alden. Remember me?"

Carrie Alden? Emma thought. *But she doesn't look anything like Carrie Alden. Carrie wasn't this thin! And Carrie didn't have hair this short. And Carrie . . .*

"Carrie?" Emma asked in a small voice.

"It's me, all right," Carrie said, a smile playing over her lips.

"But, but, you look so . . ."

"Different. Is that what you were going to say, Emma?" Carrie said.

"I guess so," Emma said.

"The gym," Carrie said simply. "And a good trainer. And a great husband."

"Billy?" Emma asked.

"Billy," Carrie echoed, a smile of happiness on her lips. "We've been married five years now. I sent you an invitation."

"I never got it," Emma said.

"Well, I sent it to your mother's," Carrie replied, one eye on Emma, and the other professionally following Kurt around the room. "It was the only address I had. Anyway, it doesn't matter."

"I'm married, too," Emma said softly, holding out her wedding ring for Carrie to see.

"To Trent what's-his-name," Carrie remarked. "I know. I saw the wedding announcement in the *Times*. You always loathed him."

117

"I know," Emma admitted, nervously twisting the huge diamond band around her finger.

"What happened?" Carrie asked.

Emma shrugged. "I used to be young and naive, I suppose. I thought marriage was what you read about in storybooks—you know, passion, love, your heart turning over with happiness when the person you love even comes into a room." Emma laughed shrilly. "Well, of course, I grew up. It really isn't anything like that at all."

"It is for me," Carrie said simply. She touched Emma's hand. "You and Kurt—"

"Oh, that was another lifetime," Emma said airily.

"But you loved him so much—"

"Well, he dropped me," Emma reminded her. "All because I couldn't cut it in the Peace Corps."

Carrie nodded. "I remember you made your father charter a private jet to fly down to Africa and bring you home."

Emma's face burned with embarrassment. "I suppose I wasn't cut out for it after all."

"I guess not," Carrie agreed.

Emma gulped hard. "No one was more disappointed in me than I was in myself."

Carrie's eyes searched Emma's face. "So you punished yourself by marrying Trent?"

"Oh, who knows?" Emma asked sharply. "Maybe Trent Hayden-Bishop III is exactly what I deserve." She took a deep breath. "Do you ever hear from Sam?"

"Sure, we see each other all the time," Carrie said. "She's out in Los Angeles. She opened her own boutique on Melrose Place. I fly out there to see her a few times a year, and she comes to New York to see me."

"That's nice," Emma said, her heart sinking. *Why is it that neither of you ever tried to see me?* she wanted to ask, but her pride wouldn't let her.

"It's a wonderful, original shop," Carrie told Emma. "Sam's brother Adam financed it after he won his Oscar for *Frank and Stein,* the low-budget movie he made that you thought was worthless."

"Really," Emma remarked, feeling worse and worse with each sentence in this conversation.

"Really! And you know—oh!" Carrie interrupted herself, "I've got to go. Job comes first! Listen, call me sometime. Next time you're in New York, we'll do lunch—or something. Good seeing you, Emma! Give my best to, uh, Trent. Bye!"

Carrie set off in search of something. Emma heard a familiar voice from behind her.

"Emma," it said.

Emma turned, and ten years of feelings flooded back into her body, leaving her short of breath and weak-kneed.

"Kurt," Emma responded huskily.

"I'm glad to see you," Kurt said quietly.

"And me, you." Emma answered.

"I've missed you."

Emma's heart swelled with hope. *Did*

he really just say he missed me? Can it really be true?

"I've missed you, too," Emma admitted.

"I always think of you," Kurt said. "Every single day of every single week."

"You do?" Emma gasped. "You really do? Even after I was such a disappointment to you?"

"Oh, yes," Kurt said. "You were young and foolish. So was I. I was much too hard on you."

Emma's heart soared with happiness. "Kurt, please don't marry Diana! I'm not happy with Trent. I can leave him! We can try again! We can—"

At that moment Diana came over to them and put her arm around Kurt's waist. "Why, it's little Emma Cresswell," she purred. "How are you?"

"Fine," Emma said stiffly.

"Really?" Diana asked, looking concerned. "Because all the color has drained from your face. You look rather sickly, dear." She turned to Kurt. "Darling, some of my friends from the Peace Corps want to give us an early wedding present. They're over by the bandstand."

"I'll be right there," Kurt assured her.

She kissed him passionately and then gave Emma a smug look. "Good to see you, Emma. I hear you're doing wonderful things with canines and felines these days."

"Yes," Emma admitted in a strangled voice.

"I guess you just weren't Peace Corps material," Diana said with a shrug. She kissed Kurt again. "Don't be long, darling."

"I have to go," Kurt told Emma.

"No, we have to talk—"

Kurt reached for Emma's hand. "It's too late for us, Emma."

"No, no, it can't be—"

"But it is," Kurt said sadly. "It's time to grow up. I'm marrying Diana."

"But you can't!" Emma cried. "My husband is having an affair with her!"

Kurt laughed. "I'm sure that's just wishful thinking on his part. After all, every man alive wants Diana. She's perfect. And as much as I miss you, Emma, Diana is my destiny."

"No! No!" Emma cried.

She was still crying "No" as Kurt walked away forever.

EIGHT

Sam's Dream

"Shut up!" Sam screamed at her alarm clock, and buried her face under her pillow. She knew what time it had to be—six A.M.—the same time the stupid alarm went off every single morning.

She reached over with one hand and threw it from the nightstand, shutting it off. Unlike most people of the twenty-first century, who had tiny vibrating alarm clocks they would fasten around their ankles before they slept, Sam still had the old-fashioned wind-up kind.

It's all I can afford, she muttered to herself, her first coherent thought of the day.

She rolled over, and then she remembered the dream she'd been enjoying just before she'd been ripped from her sleep.

God, that was the weirdest dream. So weird. I haven't thought about Emma and Carrie in such a long time. I wonder what they're doing now. I wonder if they ever think of me.

I was back on Sunset Island, Sam thought as she lay in bed for a precious extra minute before she had to get out of bed and start her seemingly endless morning routine. *We'd just had that terrible fight out on the boardwalk—the one that ended our friendship forever. But in the dream, we all made up the next day—we were all crying because we knew we had come so close to ruining the best thing any of us had ever had.*

"Sam, get up!" Allie Jacobs, now age twenty-four and a doctoral student at Kansas State University in the Social Work department, yelled to Sam from the hallway.

"Yeah, get up!" her twin sister Becky, in graduate school in the same department as Allie, intoned. "You gotta feed the kids!"

Sam groaned and stared up at the ceiling. *How could you do this to me, God?* she asked silently. *How could you have me end up with Becky and Allie Jacobs as my au pairs?*

The Jacobs twins still looked and sounded exactly alike, except now they were two very pretty, very hip young women in their mid-twenties, whom it seemed like every guy in the central Great Plains was calling on a regular basis to ask out.

"Sam, did you hear us?" Becky called again.

"I heard!" Sam shouted back. "I'll be out in a second; I'm moving as fast as I can!"

"Well, the monsters are whining and everything," Allie called in. "It's kind of obnoxious."

Sam winced when she heard Allie refer to her kids as "the monsters." *That's what I used to call Becky and Allie when I was their au pair,* she recalled. *Didn't my mother used to say something about how you reap what you sow?*

Sam sighed, got out of bed, and looked around for the ratty, shapeless muu-muu she wore just about every morning at this time. She hated it. But these days, it was about the only thing she had that she could be sure would fit her.

Just before she left her bedroom, she took a look at herself in the full-length mirror that was glued to one of the wooden doors of her clothes closet.

A twenty-nine-year-old woman stared back at her. But not a chic, fashionable, thin, hip woman in her late twenties, who once had model-thin looks and unbelievably great style.

No way. What Sam saw was a two-hundred-fifty-pound overweight woman with a very tired face, totally lifeless red hair, and too many lines around the eyes.

I look like a wreck, Sam thought, as she surveyed herself in the mirror. *Correction. I look like a fat wreck. No. Like a fat wreck who spent too much time out in the sun when she was a teenager without*

*putting enough number-fifteen sunblock
on her face though her friends told her to
all the time.*

And that's exactly how I feel.

At the moment, Sam was living in
Junction, Kansas, just down the road
from her mother and father, in a rented
three-bedroom apartment in a complex
called Toto-land Apartments. The complex featured giant cutouts of characters
from *The Wizard of Oz* strewn around the
grounds. Sam's apartment was on Wicked
Witch of the West Lane.

Sam had a part-time job as a clerk at
the local pharmacy—her boss was a guy
she had rejected in high school who now
delighted in ordering her around.

And, God help me, Sam thought, *I have
the twin au pairs from hell . . . because
no other two people would ever take the
job.*

Sam needed two au pairs. Because
Sam, four years before, had delivered a
set of triplets, whom she was now raising
single-handedly.

She touched underneath her chin and

felt the extra two chins that resided there. She lifted the wobbly flesh, trying to remember what it looked like when she had actually had a jawline.

I'm hopeless, she thought, and let the skin sag back into place. Then she took a deep breath and headed for the kitchen to start another depressing day.

"Momma, I'm hungry!" four-year old Emma cried as Sam padded into the kitchen. Emma looked like a junior version of Sam—she had flaming red hair, and she was so fat she waddled everywhere she went. She also had the biggest mouth of any four-year-old in human history.

"I know, honey," Sam said absentmindedly.

"Well, get me some grub, woman!" Emma grunted, in imitation of a character on a TV commercial.

Sam shot her child a look of distaste. *Clearly my Emma is nothing at all like her namesake,* she thought. *That Emma was perfect, and dainty, and lovely, and—*

"I'm hungry, too!" her sister Carrie chimed in.

"Me three," brother Pres added. "More hungrier than they are, those two stupid crybabies!"

"Don't call you sisters stupid," Sam said automatically as she got the milk out of the refrigerator.

"Look at this new see-through skirt," Allie said to Becky, pointing to an ad in a fashion magazine. Both twins were sitting at the kitchen table, ignoring the cacophony around them.

"Oh, yeah, cute," Becky said. She shot Sam a look. "If *someone* I know paid us decent wages, we might be able to afford a cute skirt like that."

"Maybe I'd pay you better if you decided to actually do something—like work," Sam said. "Can't you make breakfast for the kids?"

"I offered to make crepes," Allie said, not looking up from her magazine. "They didn't want crepes."

"Of course they didn't want crepes—they're four years old," Sam said, getting the cereal from the cupboard. Emma reached for the Frosted Flakes and stuck a grubby little hand in, pulling out handfuls of cereal and stuffing it into her mouth.

"Hey, I want some, too!" Carrie cried.

"Emma is a pig! Emma is a pig!" Pres sang, pointing at his sister.

"Don't call your sister a pig," Sam said automatically.

Emma stuck a half-chewed cereal-covered tongue out at her brother.

Sam looked back over at the twins. "I could use some help, here."

"Don't look at me," Becky said with a shrug. "I offered to make eggs Benedict, but they said no. They're so picky," Becky added as she took a sip of coffee.

"I want cereal!" Pres cried. He reached for Emma's Frosted Flakes and pulled hard. Emma pulled back. Finally Pres stopped pulling and Emma fell over with the cereal box, which spilled all over the floor.

"Ha-ha-ha-ha!" Pres cried gleefully. "Look what you did, you fat pig!"

"I'm not a fat pig!" Emma yelled, kicking Pres in the shins.

"Are too, are too!" Pres taunted her.

"I'm gonna cry really, really hard now!" Carrie yelled above the others.

"Hey, I want a different cereal!" Pres decided abruptly.

"Me, too!" Emma added.

"Cheerios!" Pres yelled.

"No!" Emma yelled. "I wants Lucky Stars! Lucky, lucky stars!"

"Hey, this bathing suit is cute," Allie told her sister, sliding the fashion magazine across the table again.

"Let's see," Sam said, wanting to think about fashion instead of her screaming triplets and their stupid cereal. The Frosted Flakes crunched under her feet as she leaned over.

"Sam, really," Becky laughed. "They don't make bathing suits like this in your size." She looked Sam over with distaste. "In fact, I don't think they make *any* bathing suits in your size, do they?"

"Momma, this milk is sour!" Carrie cried, sniffing the milk container.

"Ewwwwww! Disgusting! Yucky!" Pres cried. He ran out of the room gagging. Even the thought of sour milk always made him heave.

The twins were unperturbed by the racket around them. Neither made a move to get up from the picnic table that passed as a kitchen table and help in any way.

"Becky?" Sam asked, pleading. "Allie? Could you please help?" She got another carton of milk out of the refrigerator.

Both twins continued to ignore Sam, which was making her more and more angry.

"I said," Sam repeated, "can I get some help? Now! I mean it!"

"Oh, lighten up, Sam," Allie said.

Becky cracked up, and then Allie got her own unintentional joke about Sam's weight, and cracked up too. "Oops! No offense. I didn't mean that as a fat joke, I swear!"

"What Allie means," Becky said, "is that you shouldn't yell at us. Because we might just quit. And you know no *sane* person would want to work as an au pair in this house! So you wouldn't dare fire us. Right, Allie?"

"Right, Becks!"

"Who'd want to work in this dump?" Becky asked rhetorically.

"With these monsters?" Allie added, rolling her eyes. "Even your own parents don't want to have anything to do with them."

"Besides," Becky continued blithely, "this is your punishment for being so rotten to us when you were our au pair."

"And do you want to know why you're fat? Because you ragged on Erin Kane for being overweight," Allie intoned. "You thought it would be so simple for her to lose weight, and now you know just what it's like."

Then both twins stared hard at Sam and together they intoned, "Sam, you reap what you sow."

I must be dreaming, Sam thought frantically. *I have to be having some kind of hideous nightmare, and all I have to do now is wake myself up.*

Only she couldn't.

She quickly got Emma and Carrie bowls of cereal and sat them at the table, then she began to sweep up the spilled Frosted Flakes. "Could one of you go check on Pres, at least?" Sam asked.

"Nopers!" Allie replied gaily.

Sam put her hand to the small of her back and winced. "Ouch, my back is killing me."

"So go to the doctor," Becky suggested, sounding monumentally unconcerned.

"I can't afford it," Sam admitted.

"Honestly, Sam," Becky said, "everyone made a fortune during the boom at the turn of the century."

"Everyone but you," Allie noted.

Sam got a sad look on her face. What the twins were talking about was totally true. The American economy had boomed right around the year 2000 as it never had before. People all over the country were making money hand-over-fist. The stock market had soared to record heights. Finally, the American Dream had come true for a hundred million people across the land.

But I wasn't one of them, Sam thought bitterly. *For me, it was like the American Nightmare had come true. Big time.*

"This whole setup is just temporary," Sam said with bravado, pushing some of her dried, split-end hair off her face. "I'm going to change things really soon."

"Sure you are," Becky snorted derisively.

"More cereal!" Emma demanded, holding out her empty bowl. Sam filled it up and poured the milk.

"You hungry, Becks?" Allie asked her sister. She strolled over to the fridge and peered inside.

"Kind of," Becky decided.

"There's yogurt and . . . that's about it."

"We'll eat at school," Becky said with a sigh. She gave Sam a look of disapproval. "You'd better do some shopping."

"Maybe you guys could do it later," Sam asked hopefully. She wiped up some milk Emma had spilled on the table.

"No can do," Becky replied blithely. "We've got tons of work at school today, and then we've got dates."

"But you'll be able to be with the kids while I'm at work, won't you?" Sam pleaded.

"Oh, I suppose," Becky agreed irritably. "Just don't make a habit of glomming the monsters off on us, okay?"

"But that's supposed to be your job," Sam said on the verge of tears.

"Gawd, did you have to remind us?" Allie groaned. She drained her coffee.

"Sam?" Becky asked.

"Yes, Becky?" Sam asked in an exasperated tone of voice.

"Can you warm up my coffee?"

"Mine, too," Allie added, and then returned her attention to the magazine.

Sam didn't know what to do. Finally, she waddled over to the Mister Coffee— her fat thighs chafing each other with every step—and she got the coffee pot so that she could serve the twins.

NINE

Sam's Dream Continues

Sam sat in the waiting area of the Junction Community Mental Health Center and nervously flipped through a three-year-old magazine. She was about to have her first appointment with a social worker. The mental health center charged on a sliding scale and for the neediest cases was practically free.

And I am definitely one of the neediest cases, Sam thought, straightening her baggy floral-print polyester dress.

"Mrs. Angellini?" a slender, well-dressed woman in her mid-thirties called into the waiting room.

"That's me," Sam said, lumbering to her feet.

"I'm Suzanne Chaney," the woman said, shaking hands with Sam. "Please come into my office."

Sam followed the social worker into her office and sat on a tasteful green-and-white striped silk couch. The social worker sat across from Sam and crossed her slender legs.

I used to have legs like that, Sam remembered longingly. *It seems like another lifetime.*

"So, Mrs. Angellini, why don't you tell me why you're here," the social worker said pleasantly.

"Please call me Sam," Sam said.

"Fine, Sam," the social worker said. "And you can call me Suzanne. Now, what can I do for you?"

"Change my life?" Sam asked hopefully.

"I'm afraid changing your life would be up to you," Suzanne said kindly. "But perhaps I can help you do that. What is it about your life that you don't like?"

"Oh, just everything," Sam replied.

Suzanne just stared at her, waiting.

"I used to be kind of famous," Sam continued. "Well, I guess you wouldn't recognize me now. I used to be married to Johnny Angel."

Suzanne's eyebrows went up. "The rock star? He's wonderful!"

"No, he's not," Sam said flatly. "He's pond scum. His real name is Johnny Angellini—that's why you didn't recognize my last name."

"I see."

"Anyway, Johnny and I got married on the Late Night with Macauley Culkin Show—maybe you saw it—the ratings went through the roof."

"I don't usually stay up that late," Suzanne said.

"I was so happy then," Sam reminisced. "And I was thin." She sighed and grabbed a tissue from the box on the table. "Johnny started cheating on me right away. He screwed anything in a skirt. And he lied about it time and time again. Well, after he lost that third palimony suit, I couldn't take it anymore. I filed for divorce. Then he got some high-powered lawyer to trump up these charges that I was sleeping with my old boyfriend, Pres Travis—"

"*The* Pres Travis of Flirting with Danger?" Suzanne asked eagerly.

"We used to be a couple," Sam said, her throat constricting. "He's the greatest guy in the world—"

"I saw him on the Grammies last week," Suzanne said. "He's so fabulous."

"I know," Sam agreed sadly. "Anyway, this sleazoid lawyer of Johnny's made it look like I was having an affair with Pres—phony photos, a whole bunch of lies—which is how he managed to get out of paying me any alimony at all. All I get is a pittance in child support for my triplets."

"You have triplets?"

Sam nodded. "Johnny hasn't seen them since we split up. I was so depressed, I moved back home to Kansas. That's when I started gaining weight. I used to be thin! Really thin! I could eat anything I wanted! But then my metabolism changed and I turned into the Goodyear Blimp!"

"And you're unhappy," Suzanne prompted.

"No, I'm thrilled to be a fat single mother in Junction, Kansas," Sam said sarcastically.

"You're angry," Suzanne said.

"Aren't you the mental giant," Sam snorted.

"Taking your anger out on me will not be therapeutic," Suzanne said, recrossing her slender legs.

"Sorry," Sam said, chagrined. She twisted the tissue in her hand anxiously.

"So who is with your children now?" Suzanne asked.

"My au pairs, Becky and Allie Jacobs," Sam said derisively. "The funny thing is that years ago I was their au pair. They don't do any work."

"Becky and Allie Jacobs?" Suzanne echoed with excitement. "They wouldn't be graduate students in social work, would they?"

143

"They would," Sam admitted.

"Why, I'm their faculty advisor!" Suzanne cried. "I love those girls! So talented and hard-working!"

"Becky and Allie Jacobs?" Sam asked in shock.

"They mentioned that they were working for a woman who had a lot of problems—" Suzanne began, then she caught herself and stopped. "Well, I don't want to betray any confidences."

"Yeah, right," Sam snorted.

"Now, now, let's watch that anger," Suzanne chided.

"Sorry," Sam mumbled.

"Well, the way I see it is this," Suzanne said. "You have tried to succeed by leeching onto successful men instead of trying to make it on your own. You aren't a very nice person, actually, and that dress you're wearing is really hideous. It only makes you look fatter and more pathetic."

"What?" Sam asked in shock.

"I calls 'em like I sees 'em," Suzanne said with a shrug. "I mean, really, Sam, you got just what you deserve. Didn't your mother always tell you that you reap what you sow?"

"How would you know what my mother said?" Sam cried.

"Oh, I know everything," Suzanne replied smugly. She scribbled something on a piece of paper and handed it to Sam. "Here's your bill. I hope I've been helpful."

Sam looked at the piece of paper. "But this says I owe you five thousand dollars!"

"You get what you pay for," Suzanne pointed out.

"But I'm broke!" Sam yelled. "And you just insulted me and made me feel even worse than I felt when I came in here!"

"In that case you'd better come four times a week," Suzanne said. "You need a lot of help. Oh, by the way, the next time you come, could be please be a dear and bring me an autographed photo of Johnny Angel?"

*　　*　　*

145

"Sam, you didn't stock the Tampax correctly," Arnold Pishernik yelled across the drugstore to Sam. He marched over to her and brandished a box in her face. "How many times do I have to tell you we stock by absorbency—Slender to Super!"

"You don't need to advertise it to the entire store," Sam seethed in a low voice.

"Well, maybe I can embarrass you into doing a decent job!" Arnold yelled. "Nothing else does any good!"

Sam sighed and took in the pathetic sight of her boss, the general manager of Friendly Drugs. "Listen, Arnold, I know why you're so nasty to me."

Arnold crossed his arms over his massive belly. "Oh, you do, do you?"

Sam nodded. "It's because you had such a huge crush on me in high school and I didn't give you the time of day."

Arnold laughed out loud. "You're delusional."

"Oh, I don't think so," Sam replied smugly. "I was the hottest thing at Junction High. I'm sure you haven't forgotten.

146

And you were an audio-visual aid with zits."

"Sam, you were a skinny girl with no bod who everyone laughed at," Arnold corrected her.

"I was not!" Sam yelled. "I was darling! I was fabulous! I had great style!"

Arnold laughed again. "Yeah, right, like I said—delusional."

"I was once married to Johnny Angel!" Sam yelled.

"I've never believed that heap of bull," Arnold said.

"But it's true!" Sam insisted.

"Yeah, sure," Arnold said. "Well, why don't you think about ol' Johnny while you're restocking the Tampax, okay? Oh, and after that, set up a new toilet paper display, on the double."

"That ought to try my intelligence," Sam muttered sarcastically.

"What intelligence?" Arnold cracked. "You were never known for your brain."

"Neither were you," Sam shot back.

"Hey, I went to junior college!" Arnold

pointed out. "Oh, one other thing, Sam. Try to dress better when you come to work. This slovenly look doesn't cut it with Arnold P."

Sam struggled to blouse her sweat-shirt so that it wouldn't stick to her. "It's the style," Sam said loftily.

"It's the fat," Arnold countered. "You're scaring away customers."

"Look who's talking, Arnold!" Sam yelled.

"Sam, I'm your superior," Arnold in-toned. "Call me Mr. Pishernik."

"Okay, that's it, I am changing my life," Sam told herself as she drove home from work. She stopped at a light and stuffed another powdered sugar mini-doughnut into her mouth. "I can do it, I know I can do it." She washed the doughnut down with a swig of Coke she'd picked up at a fast-food place, and then ripped into the new bag of doughnuts.

Just as she was stuffing two into her mouth at once, she caught a glimpse of a cute guy in the car next to her. She gave him a flirtatious look—a look that used to have the guys flocking to her—and all she got in return was a look of disgust.

"Hey, I'm home!" Sam called when she waddled into the front door of her apartment.

"Big duh," Becky said from the couch where she was giving herself a manicure.

"Double duh," Allie echoed, applying a fresh coat of polish to her toenails. She glanced over at Sam. "Is that powdered sugar all over you, or can we add bad dandruff to your list of unsightly qualities?"

Sam brushed at her black sweatshirt, which was covered with cloyingly cute puffy paint animals. It only smeared the powdered sugar even further into the material. "It'll wash out," Sam mumbled.

"Yeah, that reminds me," Becky said, blowing on her nails, "you need to do a load of wash big time. The monsters don't have anything to wear."

"Why couldn't you do a load of wash?" Sam asked wearily.

"Surely you jest," Allie snorted.

"Where are my kids, by the way?" Sam asked.

"We ate them for lunch," Allie said.

"The fat content in Emma was unbelievable," Becky added. "But pouring on the ketchup helped."

"That is not a very funny joke," Sam said, flopping over on to the couch. "I'm tired, I'm depressed, I'm broke, and I'm hungry. And I'm not in the mood for jokes. So where the hell are my kids?"

"Children's services came and took them away," Becky said, screwing the top on her pink nail polish.

"That isn't funny, either," Sam snapped.

"I wasn't joking," Becky insisted. "They really did."

Sam's heart began to hammer in her chest. "They didn't . . ."

"They did," Allie confirmed. "Some lady insisted there had been complaints about you, that you were an unfit parent, and then they took the kids away in a big government car."

"No!" Sam screamed. "It can't be true!"

"It's true," Becky said, sounding utterly blasé about the whole thing. "We tried to call you at the drugstore but your boss said you were too busy setting up a toilet paper display to come to the phone."

"But . . . but I'm a really good mother!" Sam cried, tears coming to her eyes. "I try so hard—"

"Oh, come on," Becky chided her. "You never spend any time with them. You feed them junk food. You're a depressed wreck and a terrible mother."

"No, no, that isn't true," Sam insisted desperately. "I'm a good mother! I love my kids!"

"Liar, liar, pants on fire!" Allie chanted. "You didn't even want any kids, remember? You used to tell Emma and Carrie that you were never going to have any."

"But I was young and dumb then!" Sam cried. "Who do I have to see to get my kids back?"

"You can't," Allie said, blowing on the

new pink polish on her left hand. She held the hand out to her sister. "Hey, Becky, do you like this shade?"

"It dries too dark," Becky decided.

Sam stood up and screamed at the top of her lungs. "I don't care about your stupid nail polish! I am having a crisis! My entire life in a shambles! My kids have been taken away, I'm totally broke—"

"And fat," Allie put in helpfully. "Don't forget fat."

"And fat!" Sam added. "Please, tell me this is a nightmare and I can just wake up!"

"Nopers," Becky replied cheerfully.

She and Allie turned to Sam and stared at her. Their eyeballs disappeared, and in their place were two shining Day-Glo balls of evil; first green, then red. They both opened their mouths and formed deathlike grins, and glowing blood leaked out the side of their lips, cascading onto the olive-green shag carpet. The whole room began to fill up with blood, while Sam screamed and screamed, but no one seemed to hear her.

"You reap what you sow," the twins chanted evilly, over and over, until Sam fell into a dead faint, landing in the crimson pool of blood.

TEN

Sam's Dream Goes On

"Wha . . . what happened?" Sam said in a daze when she came to. She managed to focus her eyes on her cheap dimestore watch and realized she had passed out two hours earlier.

"Becky? Allie?" she called, lumbering to her feet. There was no answer. Then she gasped, as she remembered that the triplets had been taken away from her because she was an unfit mother. Tears came to her eyes. "They were right to take the kids!" she babbled out loud into the empty, silent room. "I really am a bad mother!"

On the cheap coffee table behind her, she noticed a note, written in Becky's handwriting, which she picked up quickly and read.

Sam,

Wow, you passed out. Bummer. Hey, you made a really, really loud noise when you fell over, no kidding. Anyway, now that the monsters are gone, there really isn't any reason for me and Allie to stick around. Of course, a deal is a deal, and we expect to get paid anyway. I mean, it isn't our fault if you messed up.

Love, Becky

"Fat chance I'm going to pay you, you lazy little worm!" Sam cried, shaking the paper in her hands the way she would have liked to shake Becky and Allie.

Then she noticed the postscript:

P.S.—
Since we know you're so cheap that you'll try to stiff us, we're sending our

buddy Bruno who is 6′ 6″, and 300 pounds of mean over to your house tomorrow to collect our money.

"Great, that's just great," Sam moaned. She stumbled into the kitchen and took out the only thing she could find in the freezer—a gallon of Rocky Road ice cream—which she took into the living room with a serving spoon. Then she sat in her favorite worn chair and clicked on the TV.

"TV will help me forget," she said to the empty room as she shoveled ice cream into her mouth.

The television—an interactive model Sam had won in a Rotary Club raffle she had entered three years before—was Sam's one and only decent possession.

Just then a familiar announcement came over the television, along with theme music that Sam knew all too well.

"Oh, thank heavens, my favorite show," Sam squealed. "This will help me put all that nastiness behind me."

She sighed with happiness, spooned

gobs of ice cream into her mouth, and sang along with the theme music:

It's grand, so grand to be famous
And it's even better when you're rich!
So come along and have some fun
On Twenty-first Century Lifestyles
  of . . .
the Rich and Famous!

"The song sucks, but the sentiment is everything," Sam pronounced, pushing the sound up higher with her remote control.

"Good evening!" the announcer with an Australian accent said, as the television showed glamorous-looking aerial shots of Hollywood, New York, Paris, London, Moscow, Beijing, and Tel Aviv. "I'm Robin Leach, Junior, and I'm pleased that you're joining me for another fabulous edition of *Twenty-first Century Lifestyles of the Rich and Famous!*"

"I'm pleased too, Robin, you betcha!" Sam yelled at the screen. She shoveled in more ice cream and sighed during the commercial for a new airline called Jet Stream, which could transport a person in deluxe luxury from New York to Europe in sixty minutes.

"Jet Stream is a Dream," the spokesmodel cooed, and Sam stuck her tongue out at the TV.

"I was cuter than you, and I could deliver a line better, too," Sam told the young woman on the screen.

Dizzying shots of the opulent lifestyles filled the screen once again, and Sam sighed at the images. *I planned to be on this show,* she remembered. *I always believed I'd succeed and be living a glamorous, fabulous life. And look at me now. Just look at me!*

As she watched the screen, Robin Leach, Jr., did a brief "Where Are They Now?" segment on the former rock star Mick Jagger of the Rolling Stones, who now was a senior citizen, and Madonna, who had found God and joined a convent, where she'd taken a vow of silence.

"Stay tuned for more *Twenty-first Century Lifestyles of the Rich and Famous!*"

Robin Leach, Jr., said, and a new commercial began.

Sam sighed and dug deeper into the ice cream, which was now melting nicely, making it easier to eat it quickly. *I was supposed to be rich and famous. Sam Bridges! ME! It's still going to happen. I know it will. I know it will!*

"We now take you to the magnificent home of the winner of the new Nobel Prize for Science," Leach intoned, his close-up filling the screen once again. "It was just announced yesterday."

"Who cares?" Sam said out loud. "I mean, big frigging deal about who won the Nobel Prize for Science. B-O-R-I-N-G!"

"She's a woman who has it all—brains and beauty! And a famous, handsome husband, too. Come, as we take you inside the life of the American scientist Emma Cresswell, on location in Kenya!"

Sam screamed and dropped her ice-cream container. *No!* she thought to herself. *This can't be happening. Not Emma! I haven't seen her since the end of that horrible summer!*

But it was Emma. Robin Leach, Jr., repeated it once for good measure.

"Ladies and gentlemen, it is my high honor to present to you, Emma Cresswell. What a special treat for *Twenty-first Century Lifestyles of the Rich and Famous!*"

Oh, my God, Sam thought, as the camera showed a long shot of Emma walking along a deserted beach, wearing a bright blue maillot swimsuit covered by a white silk shirt.

It really is her! And she looks exactly the same—perfect! She hasn't aged a day. Same perfect features, same perfect hair, and not an ounce of fat on her. And that outfit! I wish I had a silk shirt like that one.

Mesmerized, Sam leaned over and picked up the ice cream, and began shoveling it into her mouth again. She watched, a sick feeling in her stomach, as Robin Leach began a long feature on her former best friend.

He showed Emma demonstrating how she taught orangutans to play tennis, gave a guided tour around Emma's mansion outside of Nairobi, did a little feature on Emma's six-year-old son—who was already a ranked chess player—and lastly showed Emma and her French movie star husband, Pierre Le Monde, cooking a romantic French dinner together.

"Well, isn't that ducky," Sam said, scooping out the last of the ice cream and belching loudly. "She ends up with everything and I end up with nothing."

It's your own fault, a voice in Sam's head told her. *Emma was always kind, wonderful, sweet, one of the two best friends you ever had in your life, and you threw it all away.*

Sam watched as Emma fed Pierre cherries jubilee. *They look so happy!* Sam thought to herself. *Her life is so great, and mine is so miserable!*

Then Robin did a quick interview with Emma. Sam quickly pressed the "Capture" button on her nearby remote control, and a printer on the back of her TV set began to print out an instant transcript of the interview so she could read it later. As Sam watched, the printer printed silently away.

"How does it feel," Robin asked a radiant Emma, "to know that you are an inspiration to millions of girls all over the world?"

Emma blushed slightly. "I hope I'm an inspiration," she said softly. "That's a great honor."

"What's the next project you're going to undertake?" Robin asked.

"I'm teaching my orangutans to play the cello," Emma replied. "I would like to start a primate orchestra someday."

"I'm sure you will," Robin said, encouragingly. "Tell us, Emma, is there any one person who has been a special inspiration to you in your life?"

"Why yes, Robin, there is," Emma said firmly. "My best friend, Carrie Alden has always been the greatest inspiration to me."

"Hey, I was your best friend, too!" Sam wailed at the TV.

"Carrie Alden, really?" Robin asked in fascination.

Emma nodded. "Carrie is the editor-in-chief of *Rock On* magazine. Even though she's in New York, and I'm here in Kenya, we talk by videophone three, maybe even four times a day!"

"Amazing," Robin said.

"Hey! You never talk to me!" Sam cried. "And I can't afford one of those stupid videophones!"

"Carrie and I have been best friends for eleven years," Emma said happily.

"Tell him about me! Tell him about me!" Sam yelled jumping out of her seat.

"Is there anything else you'd like to say before we go?" Robin asked obsequiously. "I know you have to get back to your busy schedule of making important discoveries."

"Why, yes, Robin, there is just one more thing," Emma said. She turned and looked straight into the camera and, by extension, straight into Sam's face.

"Sam Bridges, if you're watching this—and there's no reason to doubt that you

164

are, since you always used to watch this show—you should have stuck with me and Carrie."

"Oh, my God," Sam gasped, and fell back into the chair again.

"Just look at Carrie and me now," Emma continued, still talking directly to Sam. "We're still best friends. We're both living the *Twenty-first Century Lifestyles of the Rich and Famous*. But I bet you're living in a hovel someplace with a few kids, no husband, and no life."

"She's probably fat, too," Robin added regretfully.

"Probably, Robin," Emma agreed. She turned back to the camera. "Just remember, Sam, you reap what you sow. Carrie and I made up after that fight. You never did. I bet you're sorry now."

"Yes, yes, I'm sorry!" Sam cried, burying her face in her hands. "I'm so very sorry!"

"Hmmmm," Robin Leach, Jr., commented solemnly. "Sheer profundity from a brilliant woman. Emma Cresswell. Now stay tuned for this important message."

Sam sat there, totally lost in her misery, while commercials came on for the Women's Professional Football League, a vacation junket aboard the second-generation of space shuttles, and no-fat powdered doughnuts. Sam had just enough time to scurry into the kitchen and unearth her extra large bag of potato chips from their hiding place behind the vitamins on the top shelf, then she ran back to watch the rest of the show.

"Well, ladies and gentlemen, sometimes coincidence is stranger than what we can plan, even for the rich and famous!" Robin gushed. "Our next guest just happens to be a good friend of Miss Cresswell's. We didn't plan it this way, honest we didn't!"

Then Robin pulled his right hand out of his sports jacket pocket and showed his fingers were crossed.

How dumb is that? Sam thought to herself, crunching a handful of chips into her mouth. *I could do a much better job as host than he is! All I'd have to do is*

lose eighty pounds, get my hair condi-
tioned, a few facials, a wardrobe—

"Viewers," Robin continued, "this lady wields one of the most powerful pens in showbiz. And she takes the cover photo of every issue herself. Let's go to New York to get up close and personal with the lifestyle of the incredibly rich and famous editor-in-chief of *Rock On* magazine, Carrie Alden-Sampson!"

"No! No! This can't be happening!" Sam yelled, throwing her hands over her ears. The chips flew from her lap and scattered across the rug.

The segment on Carrie opened in the offices of *Rock On* magazine—in Carrie's private office, with its incredible view of Central Park. The camera swept along the walls of the office, showing dozens of framed photographs—most of which Carrie herself had taken—of rock stars of the late twentieth and early twenty-first century. Sam quickly spotted Graham Templeton, Flirting With Danger when they'd won their first Grammy, and many others.

Then the camera moved to Carrie and Billy's Central Park West penthouse apartment, as Robin Leach, Jr., narrated the familiar story of how Carrie had been hired at *Rock On* right out of Yale and had quickly ascended to the very pinnacle of the music magazine industry in just a few short years.

There was plenty of attention given to Billy Sampson, too, along with concert footage of Flirting With Danger's performance at the thirtieth Woodstock anniversary concert several years back.

"Oh my God, it's Pres!" Sam cried, as the camera panned in on a close-up shot Carrie had taken of Pres at Anniversary Woodstock. Pres's eyes were closed in bliss as he played the bass line to the Flirts latest hit.

Sam went over to the TV screen and touched it, as if she could touch Pres's face, but too soon the camera moved on to other photos.

"I loved you, Pres," Sam whispered. "I loved you so much, and I was too young and stupid to be true to you. . . ." She wiped at the tears that fell silently down her chubby cheeks.

Then Robin switched back to the interview portion of the show. He was seated on one comfortable-looking chair in Carrie's office, and Carrie was in the other. She looked incredibly great: she'd lost fifteen or twenty pounds, had permed her hair so that it was as wild as Sam's had been eleven years before, and was wearing a South African-made black, red, and green jumpsuit that Sam had seen the day before on *Fashion Television*.

"How is it that you get all these famous people to relax for you when you take their pictures?" Robin asked Carrie.

Carrie shrugged as she spoke. "I think it's because I'm the same person I was when I was nineteen. I'm as nervous as they are!"

"That photo of Graham Perry that's in the Museum of Modern Art—is that your favorite?" Robin asked.

"No," Carrie said decisively. "My favorite is one I took of some poor people on Sunset Island in Maine ten years ago.

That's the one that started the ball rolling to help those people."

"Who's your inspiration?" Robin asked her.

"Without a doubt it is my best friend, Emma Cresswell," Carrie replied.

"Figures," Sam gulped, crying harder now.

"She's the best friend anyone could ever hope for."

"I ruined everything, Carrie!" Sam sobbed. "How could I have done it?"

"I understand from Emma that you and she have been friends for many years," Robin prompted.

"That's right," Carrie agreed. "Actually, there were three of us who were best friends back then."

"Oh, my God, she's gonna mention me!" Sam screamed.

"When Emma and I were working on Sunset Island, our other best friend was a girl named Sam—short for Samantha—Bridges."

"That's me!" Sam yelled. "I'm here! I'm watching!"

"And what happened to her?" Robin asked breathlessly.

"I don't really know," Carrie admitted. "We kind of lost touch."

"Emma's theory is that Sam is now a fat loser living alone in poverty," Robin said. "What do you think, Carrie?"

"That's probably correct, Robin," Carrie said reluctantly.

"Well, thank you, Carrie Alden!" Robin gushed. "It's been a pleasure hearing about your life."

"That's it about me?" Sam yelled. "That's all? What about how much fun I was, what excitement I brought to everyone's lives . . ."

"But enough depressing talk about a has-been loser from your past," Robin chirped, "now it's time for me to bring out a very special guest—someone you and Emma knew back then, who's a good friend now."

"Why not?" Carrie grinned.

"Viewers," Robin said, turning to the camera, "it's a pleasure to welcome to *Lifestyles* a woman whose music I'm sure

171

you love—and a good friend of our guest, Carrie Alden—Ms. Diana De Witt!"

"Kill me! Kill me now!" Sam screamed. "I can't stand it anymore!"

Diana strutted into Carrie's office, and she and Carrie hugged each other. Diana was wearing a shimmering dress of silver that barely covered her upper thighs, and silver lipstick adorned her lips, as was the latest fashion. Diana whispered some private joke in Carrie's ear, which made Carrie laugh heartily.

"The bitch looks even better than she looked ten years ago," Sam said glumly.

Robin went on and on about Diana's recently completed rock fitness video to go along with her five platinum-selling CDs.

"How's the video selling, Diana?" Robin asked, wide-eyed.

"We sold over a million copies on the first day, Robin," Diana replied.

"Well, you must be a very fit young superstar, indeed!" Robin gushed.

"Why, yes, Robin," Diana agreed. "What

with my music projects and tours, my two recent feature films—"

"Congratulations on your Oscar, by the way—" Robin interrupted.

"Thanks, Robin," Diana demurred. "That's very kind of you. Anyway, fitness is important to me."

Robin nodded seriously. "And tell us more about your work with children, Diana."

"Well, Robin, I'm sure you've heard of my learn-to-read interactive game, *Do It For Diana!*, which has taught an entire generation of preschoolers to read at age four. I'm very proud of that."

"As well you should be," Robin agreed.

Diana looked directly into the camera. "I care about children," she said, "unlike some people I know who have theirs taken away from them."

A quick retrospective on Diana's career followed: the command performances at the White House, the lead role in the latest revival of *Grease!* on Broadway, the humanitarian work with AIDS-afflicted babies, the public service announcements against drunk driving . . . then Robin brought it back to Carrie's office for the interview portion.

"Diana," Robin said, "thanks for popping in. We'll do a whole segment on you sometime soon."

"My pleasure," Diana smiled. "As soon as I get an empty minute!"

Robin laughed. "That seems like it'll be sometime in the next century!"

"I hope so," Diana said sincerely.

"Listen," Robin said confidentially, learning forward in his chair, "I understand that you and Carrie here weren't exactly friends when you first met."

"That's an understatement!" Sam hooted. "We loathed her! We called her Diana De Bitch!"

Diana leaned back and laughed heartily. "You can say that again! I hated her guts! And she hated mine, which I guess made it even."

"Ha! She actually told the truth!" Sam cackled.

"So what changed?" Robin asked.

"Nothing, nothing!" Sam yelled at the screen. "Tell the truth!"

"We all did," Carrie interjected. "Wouldn't you say so, Diana?"

"Absolutely," Diana said firmly. "I definitely changed."

"You never did!" Sam protested. "You were the same hateful witch all summer!"

"You see, Carrie and her best friend, Emma Cresswell, were big enough human beings to accept my changing," Diana said earnestly.

"We found out what a truly wonderful person Diana really is," Carrie added. "And we've been best friends with her ever since."

"It's like I always say, Robin," Diana intoned, leaning forward earnestly, "you reap what you sow." Diana turned and looked directly at Sam. "Right, Sam?"

Sam could take no more. There was a makeshift bookcase in the living room made out of boards and bricks. Sam grabbed one of the bricks from the bottom, causing the bookcase to collapse.

Then, she lobbed the brick directly at the television screen.

For once, something went right in Sam's life.

She scored a direct hit.

ELEVEN

Carrie woke up with a start, her heart hammering in her chest. She sat up and brushed the hair off her sweaty forehead.

That was one of the worse nightmares I ever had in my life, she said to herself, gulping down fresh air to still her racing heart. *And it seemed so real!*

She rushed over to the mirror to make sure she was really awake, and really eighteen years old and living on Sunset Island, instead of twenty-eight with a miserable, lonely life in New York City.

"You worked for Flash Hathaway!" she told her own reflection. "And Billy married his high-school sweetheart. And worst of all, you lost Emma and Sam forever! But it wasn't real!"

There was a soft knock on her door.

"Come on in!" Carrie called gaily. She was in a fabulous mood.

"It's me," Chloe said, sticking her head in the door.

"Hello, you," Carrie said, holding out her arms to the little girl.

Chloe ran over to her and buried her head in Carrie's arms. "I had a bad dream," Chloe mumbled tearfully.

Carrie led Chloe over to the bed and put her arm around the little girl. "Do you want to tell me about it?"

"Well, I dreamed that Ian hated me, and I was at a big birthday party, and he laughed at me."

"That's a terrible dream," Carrie commiserated.

Chloe nodded seriously. "And Mommy was mad at me, too," she continued. "In my dream she was at the party, and she was really, really nice to Ian, but she didn't even know who I was!"

"How awful!" Carrie exclaimed.

Tears rolled down Chloe's cheeks. "She said I wasn't even her little girl!"

"That was a terrible, terrible dream," Carrie said gravely.

Chloe nodded in agreement. "Yesterday I had a big fight with Ian and Mommy," she explained. "I wanted Mommy to go to the park with me, but she said she had already promised Ian she would listen to some songs he wrote, and then Ian called me a big crybaby and Mommy let him and I got so mad I said I hated her!"

Chloe's lower lip began to tremble and then she cried even harder. Carrie got some tissues, and gently wiped the little girl's face and helped her blow her nose.

"Everyone has bad dreams sometimes," Carrie said, holding Chloe close.

"Do you?" Chloe asked, looking up at Carrie.

"Oh, yes," Carrie assured her. "In fact, I had a terrible dream last night, myself."

"Really?" Chloe asked, wide-eyed. "Did you dream your mommy didn't even know you were her little girl?"

"No," Carrie replied, "but I dreamed that I was much older than I am now, and I wasn't friends with Emma and Sam anymore, even though they were friends with each other. I was so sad."

"Why did you dream that?" Chloe asked.

"Well, maybe for the same reason you had a bad dream about your mommy and Ian," Carrie said thoughtfully. "I had a fight with them yesterday, and I went to sleep feeling very badly about it."

"Were they mean to you?" Chloe wondered.

"Maybe," Carrie said. "But maybe I was mean to them, too." She sighed deeply and looked out the window. The sun had just risen, the birds were singing—it was a beautiful morning. *But it wouldn't be worth anything at all if I lost Sam and Emma,* Carrie realized.

She looked back at the little girl fondly. "Anyway," she continued, "the important thing is that when you have a fight with someone you love, you have to make sure that you make up with them as soon as you can. Because the longer you wait to say I'm sorry, the harder it is to say it."

Chloe nodded seriously. "Yeah," she whispered.

"It's so important," Carrie said passionately, talking to herself at least as much as she was talking to Chloe. "Nothing is worth the risk. . . ."

Chloe blew her nose again. "Carrie?"

"What, sweetie?"

"When I told Mommy I hated her," Chloe began, "I didn't mean it."

I didn't mean half the things I said yesterday, either, Carrie realized. "I know you didn't, sweetie," Carrie told the little girl. "And your mommy knows it, too."

"But I still want to tell her," Chloe insisted. "And I want to tell Ian, too."

"I think that's a wonderful idea," Carrie agreed.

Chloe looked up at Carrie. "Do you think they're still mad at me?" she asked in a small voice.

Carrie hugged the little girl's shoulders. "I think they both love you very, very much," she said. "And I think they'll both be very happy to hear you say you're sorry, and to have you tell them how much you love them."

Chloe nodded. "Okay, I will." She cocked her head at Carrie. "Are you going to tell Sam and Emma you're sorry?"

"Absolutely," Carrie said. "I'm just hoping they love me as much as your mommy and Ian love you."

"How come?" Chloe asked.

Carrie gulped hard. "So that they'll give me a second chance, Chloe."

"Kurt! Kurt! Come back!" Emma yelled. "I love you!"

"Diana is my destiny," Kurt repeated in an eerie voice. "It could have been different, a long time ago. But now it's too late, too late, too late, too late . . ."

Emma gasped and sat up in bed. "No!" she cried. "It can't be too late! It can't!"

She looked around the darkened room and let her pulse slow down. *I'm here at the Hewitts,* she told herself. *I'm not married to Trent. Kurt isn't marrying Diana.* Then her breath caught in her chest. *But I really did have a terrible fight with Carrie and Sam,* she remembered. *I really could lose their friendship!*

Emma glanced over at the clock. It was only four o'clock in the morning. *It's too early to call either of them,* she realized. *I wish I could tell them right this second how stupid we all were! I wish I could tell them how sorry I am about the fight!*

She sighed and swung her legs over the end of the bed. *I'll never be able to fall back asleep, and I can't call them for at least three hours,* she thought. *I'll go for a bike ride to the beach and clear the nightmare from my head.*

Quickly Emma washed her face, brushed her teeth, and threw on some old sweats, then as quietly as possible went downstairs, got a bicycle out of the garage, and headed for the ocean.

The boardwalk was deserted when she got there, and Emma was glad for the solitude. She ran down to the edge of the water and looked out at the sunrise, breathing hard. *Another day and another chance,* she thought to herself, as she watched the fiery ball rising over the ocean. A gull called and swooped into the water, silhouetted in the half-light. Emma breathed in the salt air deeply and hugged herself hard. *Another day, another chance.*

"Hi," called a voice behind her.

Emma was startled. She turned around and saw Darcy Laken standing there.

Darcy was a good friend of Emma, Sam, and Carrie's. She was tall, muscular and athletic, with long black hair. She was tough and plain-speaking, too, which Emma really appreciated. And she also had a touch—well, maybe more than a touch—of ESP.

"Hi," Emma said. "I didn't know anyone else was around."

"I just got here," Darcy explained. "I guess my bare feet didn't make much noise in the sand." She took a couple of steps toward the ocean and looked out. "Beautiful sunrise, huh?"

Emma nodded. "I don't get to see it very often. Do you?"

"No," Darcy said. "I'm definitely a sleep-until-the-last-possible-moment kind of girl." She turned to Emma. "But I had a dream that woke me up. And here I am."

"I had a dream, too," Emma said with a shudder. "A terrible one."

"I know," Darcy said simply, pushing some windblown hair off her face.

"You do?" Emma exclaimed. "But how?"

"It was really bizarre," Darcy admitted. "I was twenty-nine instead of nineteen, and you, Sam and Carrie were all twenty-eight or twenty-nine—"

"That's what I dreamt, too!" Emma gasped.

"I could see all of you," Darcy continued, "but none of you could see me. And the three of you were so unhappy, and none of you were friends—"

"That's just like my dream! Only Carrie and Sam were friends, but I was just a faint memory to them."

"I kept trying to tell you all that it wasn't too late," Darcy said earnestly, "that if you really loved each other, you could still apologize and find one another again—"

"And what happened?" Emma asked eagerly.

"None of you could hear me," Darcy said sadly. "You couldn't see me and you couldn't hear me."

Emma reached down to pick up a seashell, which she threw out into the ocean. "You're amazing, Darcy," she marveled. "You hooked into my dream somehow."

"Not just yours," Darcy said thoughtfully. "At least, that's the feeling I had."

"You mean . . ."

Darcy nodded. "I mean Sam and Carrie had terrible dreams about the future, too."

"Theirs couldn't have been as bad as mine," Emma said with a shudder. "I was married to my old boyfriend, Trent. I can't stand him. And Kurt was marrying Diana!"

"That's a fate worse than death," Darcy said with an ironic chuckle.

"It was so awful!" Emma cried. "I had finally gotten my chance to be in the Peace Corps, and I went to Africa, just like I've always dreamed. But I went

186

home after two weeks because I couldn't handle the hard work. I was a sniveling, obnoxious little rich girl—oh, it was awful!"

"Sounds like it," Darcy agreed.

"I had turned into exactly the kind of person I can't stand," Emma shuddered. "I had turned into someone like my *mother*!"

"Bad dream," Darcy commiserated.

"Why would I dream that?" Emma mused.

"Have any theories?" Darcy asked curiously.

"Just the obvious," Emma replied. "Last summer Kurt slept with Diana—" The words caught in Emma's throat. "It still hurts, even now."

"It probably always will," Darcy allowed.

"Kurt and I broke up. I never thought we'd get back together, and I never thought I'd be able to forgive him—"

"Have you?" Darcy asked.

"I thought I had," Emma admitted.

She dug the toe of her Nike into the sand thoughtfully.

"Sometimes dreams bring out whatever we feel most insecure about," Darcy said. "At least that's what my psych professor says."

"Meaning that I feel insecure about Diana," Emma admitted in a low voice. She sighed and looked out at the sea. "I suppose I do—although I would never in a million years admit that to her." She turned to look at Darcy. "But why would I dream that my life was so horrible— empty and vacuous, just like my mother's—and that I had lost Sam and Carrie's friendship?"

"I guess you dreamed about your greatest fears," Darcy suggested.

"I can't imagine what it would be like to be you," she told Darcy. "To actually dream about the future. . . ."

"It sounds much cooler than it actually is sometimes," Darcy said. She sighed deeply. "Sometimes I've had dreams that something bad was going to happen to someone, and I couldn't stop it from happening . . ."

"And then it actually happened," Emma finished for her.

Darcy nodded. "So doesn't that make me kind of responsible, in a way?"

"I don't know," Emma said honestly. "But it sounds like a huge burden."

"Yeah, it *feels* like a huge burden, too," Darcy agreed.

Emma bit her lower lip. "Do you think . . . I mean, was your dream last night something that is fated to happen to me and Carrie and Sam in the future? God, that would be so terrible—"

Darcy put her hand on Emma's arm. "I think you can change it."

"But you said yourself that sometimes you dream about the future, and then whatever you dreamed about actually happens—"

"And sometimes it doesn't," Darcy put in earnestly.

Emma stared at her friend. "This is in my power to change."

Darcy nodded. "I think so."

The sun had risen above the horizon; the sky shone a clear, pale blue. Emma was surprised to see a little girl on a pink bike at that hour. She was making zig-zags across the boardwalk behind them, her mother running after the bike. "I can do it, Mom! Without training wheels!" she cried happily.

"I can do it, too," Emma vowed. "I can make my own future, and it will be totally different than that terrible dream."

"Cool," Darcy said with a grin.

Emma grinned back at her friend. "Thanks, Darcy."

"Hey, what are strange friends with ESP for?" she asked lightly.

Emma hugged her quickly. "For helping me see what's really important, that's what. You're the greatest."

"Sam! Wake up! Wake up!"

Sam opened her eyes and stared up at Becky and Allie Jacobs, who were leaning over her bed.

"You came back!" Sam cried.

Becky gave her a funny look. "We never left."

"Yes, you did," Sam insisted. "You quit!"

"Sam, did you get too much sun yesterday or something?" Allie asked, peering down at Sam. "You were, like, totally screaming in your sleep. It's only five o'clock in the morning."

"Did you have a weird dream or something?" Becky asked.

Sam's eyes grew huge and she sat up slowly. Then she reached down and felt her stomach, then her hips. Then she lifted the quilt and looked at her body, clad only in a Sunset Island T-shirt. "I'm not fat!" she screamed joyfully.

The twins traded looks. "She's really lost it," Becky told her sister.

"I'm thin!" Sam shrieked.

"You're skinny, actually," Allie corrected.

"Yes! I'm skinny!" Sam yelled. "And I don't have triplets!"

"Triplets?" Becky shrieked.

"And you two don't work for me!"

"Get a grip, Sam," Allie snorted. "You work for us."

191

"Oh, I'm so happy!" Sam screamed. She threw back the covers and ran over to the dresser to look at herself in the mirror. "It was all just a terrible dream!"

"You dreamed you were fat and had triplets and we worked for you?" Allie asked incredulously.

Sam nodded. "You were my au pairs, but you never did any work, and I was divorced from Johnny Angel and I was fat and poor and lonely—" Sam babbled.

"Whoa, back up," Becky commanded. "You were divorced from Johnny Angel? That means you dreamed you had been actually married to him, which means you would have had sex with him . . . that's the part we want to hear about."

"Oh, God, the worst part was that I wasn't friends with Carrie and Emma anymore!" Sam recalled, ignoring the twins.

Allie looked at her sister. "I have a feeling she's not gonna give us any juicy stuff about Johnny Angel."

"Figures," Becky said with a sigh. "Come on, Allie, let's go back to sleep."

Before the twins could make it out the door, Sam ran over and hugged them both hard. They stood there, stunned.

"I love you guys!" Sam cried. "I'm just so happy to be me, and nineteen, and on Sunset Island!"

"Yeah, uh . . . great," Becky said, backing toward the door.

"Sure, we're real happy for you, too, Sam," Allie agreed, also heading for the door. "See ya!" They escaped quickly.

"Bye!" Sam called. "I'll make anything you guys want for breakfast later!" she yelled after them. Sam looked in the mirror again and hugged herself hard. *I have to do something wonderful for Carrie and Emma,* she thought to herself. *I have to show them how much they mean to me.*

Just then her eyes lit on a bunch of rhinestone pins she'd been planning to use for her latest batch of Samstyles, and a huge grin spread across her face.

I know just the thing, Sam thought. *Sometimes actions really do speak louder than words. . . .*

TWELVE

They'll come. I know they'll come, Sam told herself as she paced back and forth on the boardwalk in front of Wheels, a bicycle rental store. She looked at her Mickey Mouse watch for the tenth time in five minutes. *My note said eight o'clock, and it's still ten to eight. What if they're still sleeping? I'm just nervous. . . .*

"Well, shut my mouth," a masculine, southern voice drawled. "Sam Bridges, out on the boardwalk early in the A.M. Is it a miracle?"

Sam turned around. "Pres," she said with a happy grin.

He came over to her and wrapped his long arms around her in a quick hug.

"Good morning, you sweet thing. What are you doin' up and about?"

"Meeting Carrie and Emma," Sam replied. "At least, I hope I'm meeting them. I left notes at their houses this morning. . . . I hope they read them when they got up to help with breakfast."

Pres's eyebrows shot up. "You mean to tell me you've already been around to their houses?"

"Yep."

"What did you do, girl, not go to bed last night?" Pres said with a laugh. "Because I know my baby hates getting up early."

"You're right," Sam agreed. She leaned against the wooden rail with her elbows. "But the three of us had a fight last night, and then I had this terrible nightmare about my life ten years from now. They weren't even my friends anymore!"

"Ten years into the future, huh?" Pres mused, scratching at his chin. "Was I in this dream?"

"No," Sam admitted. "I was divorced

from Johnny Angel. And I had triplets. And I was fat!"

Pres threw his head back and laughed. "Now, if there is one thing I can't imagine, it's you fat!"

"Well, I was!" Sam exclaimed. "You know how everyone always tells me that my metabolism is going to change one day and I won't be able to eat like a pig without gaining weight? Well, that's exactly what happened!"

"Lord, Lord, Lord," Pres said, still laughing, "that was quite a nightmare."

"Yeah, well, it was quite a fight." Sam sighed. "I was ticked at Carrie about Billy."

"About Billy?" Pres echoed. "But it's not her fault he had to go to Seattle—"

"I know that," Sam agreed. "But I said I thought the Flirts should be able to go on without Billy. I said I didn't think it was fair to just keep everyone hanging—"

"Sam, if the Flirts want things to change, then the Flirts can vote to do something different," Pres pointed out.

"But unless Jake and Jay and me decide to go on without Billy, we'll be waiting."

"But it's so hard for you!" Sam exclaimed. "I know how much the band means to you—"

"Sam, I can handle my own battles," Pres said gently. "This one ain't yours."

"Meaning I'm only a backup singer and I should know my place," Sam translated.

"Meaning Billy and I started the Flirts together," Pres explained. "And I can hang in awhile longer." He lightly touched Sam's arm. "Anyway, it sure wasn't worth fighting about with your best friends, was it?"

"I don't know," Sam said. "Maybe it was." She turned around and leaned against the rail again, looking out at the ocean in the distance. "But I was thinking. No matter how much you love someone, there are still times that you disagree, right?"

"Right," Pres agreed, leaning against the rail with Sam.

"I mean, you can love someone and

have a disagreement—even a fight, right?" Sam pressed.

"Right."

Sam nodded. "And it's so easy to let a fight get out of control, you know what I mean? It just gets bigger and bigger, until it seems bigger than love or respect or . . . or just anything!"

Pres nodded and put his arm around Sam's shoulders. "That's right, too," he agreed.

"Yeah, well, I guess that's what happened with us last night," Sam explained.

"I remember my momma had a friend who hadn't spoken to her brother in something like twenty years," Pres recalled. "She told me about it one day when she was over to dinner. She said they had had a fight. And I asked her. 'What was that fight about that made you not speak to your brother for twenty years?' And she said, 'Pres, I don't remember.'"

Sam shuddered. "I don't want to be that stupid."

Pres leaned over and kissed Sam on

the cheek. "You won't be," he told her. "Well, I gotta git. I'm doing inventory at Wheels this morning."

"Can I have a better kiss than that before you go?" Sam asked.

Pres put his arms around her waist and moved closer. "Ouch!" he cried, jumping back. "What bit me?"

"This pin I have on," Sam explained.

Pres looked at it more carefully. "S-E-C in rhinestones?"

Sam nodded. "I'll explain it to you sometime." She held up her arms and wrapped them around his neck.

This time he was careful of her pin. He kissed her slowly and deeply. "How's that?"

"Perfect," Sam said with a sigh. "Just perfect."

Pres felt Sam's ribcage. "You were fat, huh? I bet you were cute, all plumped up—"

Sam swatted his hands away. "I wasn't."

He kissed her quickly and walked away from her backward. "I bet I would have thought you were cute. I'll call you." He looked down the boardwalk, where

Carrie and Emma were quickly making their way toward Sam, and he gave Sam a thumbs-up sign before disappearing into Wheels.

"Hi," Emma said breathlessly. "I picked Carrie up."

"Hi," Sam said. And then a huge grin spread across her face. "You got them."

Carrie and Emma exchanged grins. "They're fabulous," Carrie said.

Carrie was dressed in jeans and a sweatshirt, and Emma had on cutoff jeans and a white T-shirt, and both of them wore rhinestone pins exactly like Sam's. She had taken the backing off some larger rhinestone pins and then super-glued tiny rhinestones to it to form the letters S-E-C. Then she had taken the pins to Emma and Carrie's employers' homes and had left the pins, along with a note-asking them to meet her, on their front porches.

"I know the two of you aren't exactly rhinestone types—" Sam began.

"There's an exception to every rule," Carrie said firmly. She pointed to the S on her pin. "I noticed you got top billing," she added with mock severity.

"For a good reason, though, as opposed to my unbridled ego," Sam replied. "It spells SEC, as in second. As in a reminder that next time I should wait a second before I open my mouth and say something really stupid that I regret."

"Speaking of regrets," Emma began. "I—"

"No, let me," Sam said, interrupting. "I have to tell you guys and it can't wait. I had the worst nightmare—"

"Me, too!" Carrie exclaimed.

"Me, too!" Emma added. "Wow, Darcy was right!" Her friends stared at her. "I saw her early this morning when I went for a run on the beach. She had a nightmare, too, that all of us were ten years older and weren't even friends anymore—"

"In my dream, you and Emma were friends," Sam said, "and I was all alone."

"No!" Carrie cried. "You and Emma were friends, and *I* was all alone!"

"But I dreamed that you two were

friends, and you barely even remembered me!" Emma said. "But the very worst thing was about Diana. She was—"

"Best friends with both of you!" they all said at the same time. Then they all cracked up, falling over themselves with laughter. Each of them told the other two what she had dreamed. When they finished, they all just looked at each other with wonder.

"Wow, this is mondo-bizarro, don't you think?" Sam asked.

"It's pretty strange," Carrie agreed.

"It's funny, isn't it?" Emma mused. "We all dreamed that the other two were successful, with wonderful, happy lives, and we were all alone and miserable."

"That's not going to happen . . . is it?" Sam asked, in a small voice.

"It's because of the fight," Emma said in a low voice.

"We never fight," Carrie pointed out.

"Oh, look, we're human!" Sam said. "I mean, we're not joined at the hip, you know? We have different ideas about things. . . ."

"But how did we let it get so ugly last night?" Emma wondered.

"I don't know," Sam said. She fingered her rhinestone pin. "But this will remind me to think before I speak . . . I hope."

"You know, it really is okay if we disagree about things sometimes," Carrie pointed out.

"Why does it feel so personal, though?" Emma wondered.

"I don't know," Sam admitted. "It's dumb." She thought about the story Pres had told her about his mom's best friend who hadn't spoken to her brother for twenty years, and she told Emma and Carrie.

"That's awful," Emma said passionately. "That would never happen to us!"

"But it could," Carrie pointed out, "if we were stupid."

Sam's face paled. "You don't think those dreams were, like, looking into the real future, do you?"

"What could be, maybe," Emma said, "not what has to happen."

"Kind of like a warning," Sam agreed.

She put her hands on her stomach. "God, I was fat! Huge! Gigundo! I lived in a muu-muu!"

"We all dreamed about our worst insecurities and our worst fears coming true," Carrie said.

Emma nodded. "But why did we all dream that Diana ended up with everything she ever wanted? No, worse than that, we all dreamed that she ended up with everything *we* ever wanted!"

"Well, I guess that's our worst fear," Carrie said.

Sam thought a moment. "Do you think life is fair?"

"No," Carrie said bluntly. "I wish it was, but I know it's not."

"Yeah, I guess," Sam agreed slowly. "Which means that Diana De Witt, the She-Devil From Hell, really could end up living happily-ever-after, just like in our dreams."

"Well, speaking of the she-devil," Carrie said, cocking her head down the boardwalk. "Isn't that Diana?"

Emma and Sam both turned to look.

"Wow, she looks awful!" Emma exclaimed. She turned to Sam. "Does she still think she's pregnant?"

Recently, at a bonfire on the beach, Diana had blurted out to everyone that she was pregnant. She had actually confided in Sam, and Sam had kept her secret. Then Sam had explained that Diana didn't know for sure yet, because it was too early for her to take a pregnancy test.

Sam shrugged. "I don't know. I haven't talked to her in days." She peered at Diana as she got closer. "She really does look like dogmeat."

As Diana came closer, the girls saw that she had on dirty jeans and a denim shirt that was missing a button. Her usually perfectly groomed hair was dull and greasy looking. There were dark circles of mascara under her eyes. She didn't have on any other makeup, and her skin looked pasty even under her tan.

"Hi," Diana said in a flat voice when she reached them. "How nice of the three of you to show up to wish me a good morning."

"That remark lacks your usual venom," Carrie pointed out.

"It's too early for venom," Diana said, holding her head.

"Are you . . . okay?" Emma asked delicately.

"If you mean am I pregnant, the answer is none of your business," Diana snapped.

"Diana, you made it everyone's business when you blurted it out at the bonfire," Carrie reminded her.

"Oh, thank you very much, Carrie Alden," Diana spat. "You are such a helpful little Girl Scout."

Carrie sighed.

"I had the worst nightmare last night," Diana groaned. "It was a dream about the future. I had lost my looks, and I was poor—I was on welfare!" She looked around at the three girls. "And you were all there!" she recalled. "And you were rich! And gorgeous! And successful! And I was eating dog food out of a can!"

"Boy, that's a video I'd pay big money for," Sam smirked.

"Wait a second," Carrie said. "You had this dream last night?"

Diana nodded. "You were a famous photojournalist," she told Carrie. "And you were director of the Peace Corps," she told Emma. "And you . . ." she said, pointing at Sam, "you were a rock star who went by one name, like Madonna!" Diana declared, clearly aghast at the thought.

"I love this!" Sam screamed. "This is the best!"

"And Lorell Courtland—*my* best friend—was now best friends with the three of you, and she didn't even know I existed!" Diana continued, fear and loathing written across her face.

"You're kidding," Emma exclaimed. Diana had had the same kind of horrible nightmare the three of them had had! Emma, Carrie and Sam looked at each other and broke out laughing. It was too much to believe.

"You know, the three of you are really

sick!" Diana yelled at them. "How can you get joy out of someone else's misery?"

"No, you don't understand," Sam started to explain, tears of laughter running down her cheeks. "You see—"

"I never should have told you," Diana said. Her eyes narrowed. "No one laughs at Diana De Witt and gets away with it! The three of you will live to regret this," she vowed.

"Oh, come on, Diana," Carrie said. "Lighten up. No one forced you to tell us about your dream. And you have to admit—it *is* funny!"

"No, Carrie," Diana replied in a frosty voice. "I don't think it's funny. Funny would be a dream where you were eating dog food and I was making out with Billy in Seattle."

"Dream on," Carrie sang out, only too aware of how close Diana was to pinpointing her own nightmare fears.

Just at that moment Diana held her stomach and got a panicked look on her face. Then her cheeks puffed up and she ran out onto the beach and heaved.

"Do you need some help?" Sam called to Diana.

"No!" Diana yelled back.

"We should go help her anyway, shouldn't we?" Emma wondered. "Diana?" She started.

"Go to hell!" Diana screamed.

The three of them looked at each other for a moment.

"I guess she doesn't want any help," Carrie said with a shrug.

The sounds of Diana throwing up got louder.

"Feel better, Diana!" Sam called out.

The three girls walked in silence for a few minutes, enjoying the clean morning air and the sun on their shoulders.

"I love it here," Emma finally said in a low voice.

Carrie nodded. "I do, too," she agreed. "But if I lost the two of you . . ."

"All the joy would be gone," Sam filled in. "Right?"

"Right," Carrie agreed. "All the joy would be gone." She looked over at Sam. "I can't apologize for disagreeing with you last night, Sam, but I'm sorry I let it turn into what it turned into."

"Me, too," Sam said. "We don't have to agree about everything, right?"

"Right," Emma said. "And we have to remember that our friendship is bigger than that."

Sam sighed. "Most people who say they'll stay friends never do, you know."

"We're different," Carrie insisted.

"Are we?" Sam asked plaintively. "I want to believe that."

"We *are* different," Emma said firmly. "It's like . . . I feel as if those dreams meant something, you know? It was as if my mind was telling me that with the two of you as my best friends, I can succeed in ways that I never could without you."

"Yeah," Sam said, "like the three of us together are stronger than any of us alone, something like that."

"Something like that," Carrie agreed, smiling at Sam.

"Hey," Sam said, and she stopped walking and put her hand on her hips. "Do you think that Diana had that dream that she was poor and lonely because she's really insecure?"

"Sam, I think deep down everyone is insecure," Carrie replied.

"Yeah, right," Sam snorted. "No one is as insecure as I am. You look up insecure in the dictionary, you find my mug shot."

"And mine," Emma admitted.

"And mine," Carrie added. "And I'll bet Diana's, too. And for her sake I actually hope Lorell is back on the island."

"Huh," Sam marveled. "Who would have thunk it." She stretched her arms up to the sky and pulled the kinks out of her back. "You know, it's going to be a gorgeous day," she said happily. "And I am one babe who is happy to be alive." Her stomach growled out loud. "I'm also starving." She felt her narrow waist. "I'm thin and starving! Yes! I can go eat whatever I want!"

"Reality is pretty good, huh?" Carrie teased her.

"Reality is pretty great," Sam agreed. She looked at the SEC pins on Carrie and Emma's shirts. "Did I mention that the two of you have fabulous taste in jewelry?"

They all reached up and touched their pins at the same time.

"It's an original," Emma said softly.

"Kind of like us," Sam said brightly. She hooked one arm through Carrie's, and one through Emma's, and then, just like Dorothy, the Tin Woodsman, and the Scarecrow in *The Wizard of Oz*, the three of them danced into the future.

SUNSET ISLAND MAILBOX

Dear Readers,

Yes, the fan mail is flying into my mailbox. You guys would really laugh if you saw my office: floor-to-ceiling letters and two walls covered with photos of all you incredible Sunset sisters out there! Oh, and of course, a photo of Jeremy Thompson, my fave guy fan from Jasper, Alabama. Jeremy watch update: He's going to college this fall, but promises to keep answering all the letters you guys write to him. He's gotten tons of mail already from all over the country. He wrote to tell me he's very impressed at how cool, smart, funny and terrific the letters have been. Just remember, if you want to write to Jeremy, send your letter to me but also put his name on it, and I will forward it unopened to him.

Lately I've actually been getting more mail from guys (but we all know Jeremy was the first!), and they tell me that SUNSET books let them in on the real deal with girls. Well, of course! Do you think we should let them keep reading? Are there any messages you want me to get across to the guys of America? Just let me know!

FAN UPDATE . . . I had lunch recently with Marci Robinson—a total sweetheart, by the way—who drove all the way to Nashville from Michigan just to meet moi—hey, I was honored! In July I'm expecting a visit from Carrie Schnarr of Indiana. I love meeting you guys; if you're going to be in Nashville, give me a call! Great mail and photos recently from Melanie Moore of Tecumseh, Michigan (love those glamour shots!); Alissa Hebert of Raceland, Louisiana (what a cutie!); darling Heidi

Carter and her guy (oops, ex-guy—time marches on) Jared Vincent of Nachitoches, Virginia; Ashley Bellingham of Milwaukee, Wisconsin (love your hair!); and Erica Kramer of Ormond Beach, Florida, who sent me photos of her cute self with *every single book I have ever written!* As Sam would say, "Whoa, baby!"

So, you know how much I love to hear from all of you, right? I get so many great ideas from your heartfelt letters. I hope your lives are terrific—although, believe me, I know there are always ups, downs and sideways. I am always here for you, always ready to listen. But enough mush—you know I care.

See you on the island!
Best -
Cherie Bennett

Cherie Bennett
c/o General Licensing Company
24 West 25th Street
New York, New York 10010

Dear Cherie,
Hi, I'm a sixteen-year-old girl, and your last book I read was Sunset Heart. I was really touched by this book—it helped me out a lot. I had sex with this guy who had not always been safe. Someone said he had AIDS, so I got my best friend to take me to get tested. Thank the Lord, I am negative. But as I look back on that night, I know how stupid I was for having sex with him. I'm too young to die from being stupid and not thinking

clearly. I just wanted you to know how much I appreciated Sunset Heart. *I know I'm not the only one who feels this way.*

> *Sincerely yours,*
> *M.P.*
> *Crenshaw, Mississippi*

Dear M.P.,

Thank you for being brave enough to share your very personal story with me and with your Sunset sisters. You got it exactly right— it is so important to think clearly, even in a situation where your heart or your hormones are telling you otherwise! <u>Sunset Heart</u> has gotten a lot of attention. One book critic even said that the president of Berkley Books should get an award for having published it, because it is so timely! I am happy that your AIDS test was negative, but please make sure that you get tested again six months after your first test. It is extremely important.

> Best,
> Cherie

Dear Cherie,

Sunset Island *rocks! Long live Sam! I'm so glad Diana is out of the Flirts, and I'm so sad about Sly. Next time I write, I'll enclose a movie review I wrote. What's your favorite movie?*

> *Love,*
> *Heather Wadowski*
> *Northville, Michigan*

Dear Heather,

It's great that you're writing movie re- views. I tell a lot of teens who ask me about how to make a career out of writing nonfiction that they should try to write movie reviews or theater reviews for their school papers. Also, it's sometimes possible to get your local newspaper to let you review a play or movie from a teen's point of view. A lot of critics got their start that way! I'll tell you two movies I liked a lot that didn't get a lot of attention when they were released, but are available at your local video store. One is called <u>Dominick and Eugene</u>, and the other is called <u>A Midnight Clear</u>. Check them out!

Best,
Cherie

Dear Cherie,
I recently started reading your books, and I love them! I think they teach a lot about friendship, and they're a lot of fun. I'm probably most like Sam. I'm pretty tall for my age, with red hair. This might seem a little weird, but do you ever get up in the middle of the night and write ideas down?
Your friend,
Jessica Boche
Muscatine, Iowa

Dear Jessica,
Great question! Actually, the best time for me to get ideas is right before I fall asleep. Most of the time, I remember in the morning. But not always! When that happens it's really maddening, and I always vow that next time I'll write my ideas down. Not that I've actually kept my vow yet—well, who ever said I was perfect?

Best,
Cherie